D1541671

Essential Histories

The Zulu War 1879

Essential Histories

The Zulu War 1879

Ian Knight

OSPREY
PUBLISHING

First published in Great Britain in 2003 by Osprey Publishing, Elms Court, Chapel Way, Botley, Oxford OX2 9LP
Email: info@ospreypublishing.com

ISBN 1 84176 612 7

A CIP catalogue record for this book is available from the British Library

Editor: Sally Rawlings
Design: Ken Vail Graphic Design, Cambridge, UK
Cartography by The Map Studio
Index by David Worthington
Picture research by Image Select International
Origination by Grasmere Digital Imaging, Leeds, UK
Printed and bound in China by L. Rex Printing Company Ltd.

03 04 05 06 07   10 9 8 7 6 5 4 3 2 1

For a complete list of titles available from Osprey Publishing please contact:

Osprey Direct UK, PO Box 140,
Wellingborough, Northants, NN8 2FA, UK.
Email: info@ospreydirect.co.uk

Osprey Direct USA, c/o MBI Publishing, PO Box 1,
729 Prospect Avenue, Osceola, WI 54020, USA.
Email: info@ospreydirectusa.com

www.ospreypublishing.com

Contents

Introduction   7

Chronology   9

Background to war
The Zulu kingdom   11

Warring sides
Fight us in the open   19

Outbreak
British invasion plans   26

The fighting
The January battles   28

Portrait of a soldier
Fighting for the empire   58

The world around war
Reaction to the war   66

Portrait of a civilian
Zulu attitudes towards the war   69

How the war ended
Renewed offensives   74

Conclusion and consequences
Pacifying Zululand   82

Further reading   92

Index   94

Introduction

The Anglo-Zulu War of 1879 remains one of the best-known 'little wars' in the history of the later British Empire. Nearly 125 years after the last shots were fired, it still inspires a constant stream of feature films, TV documentaries, articles – popular and academic – and books. In the last 10 years, a small but vibrant industry has grown up catering for the steady trickle of tourists who make their way to the remote battlefields in South Africa. In many ways, it is of course easy to understand the war's popular appeal. Within days of British troops crossing the Zulu border, a British camp was overrun at the foot of Isandlwana hill in a military disaster almost unparalleled in the Victorian era. Yet this defeat was followed immediately by the spirited defence of the border post at Rorke's Drift, an incident which restored the British public's faith in their armed forces in the light of the earlier embarrassment, and which made popular heroes of the small garrison – as, remarkably, they have remained ever since. The dramatic juxtaposition of victory and defeat has an apparent symmetry which has allowed both sides some comfort over the years. As one Zulu once put it to me on the battlefield at Isandlwana, 'We both lost our away matches; but won our home games!'

Yet the apparent glamour which still attaches to the war is deeply misleading. For all its cinematic qualities – the colourful African warriors pitched against red-coated soldiers against a backdrop of majestic landscapes and big skies – the war was a brutal one which resulted ultimately in the dispossession of an African people. It lasted for six months, and in that time the opposing armies fought no fewer than eight significant engagements. Nearly 20,000 British and colonial troops and their African allies took part in the war, as did perhaps 40,000 Zulus. Some 2,000 British and allied troops died in combat or of disease, while perhaps as many as 10,000 Zulus were killed. Since the Zulu army was not a full-time professional organisation, in the manner of the British Army, but rather the manpower of the nation gathered together temporarily for military duties, the impact of these casualties affected all areas of Zulu society. By the end of the war, the Zulu king, Cetshwayo kaMpande, had been captured by the British and deposed, and in a deliberate attempt to break up the kingdom's administrative structure most of the great royal homesteads had been destroyed. Thousands of head of cattle belonging to the Zulu state and ordinary civilians alike were looted by the British, and hundreds of family homesteads razed to the ground.

King Cetshwayo kaMpande. Cetshwayo's accession in 1873 coincided with a gradual shift towards a more expansive policy among Zululand's British neighbours, which culminated in the conflict of 1879. (Ron Sheeley Collection)

Ironically, the attention which the war still commands belies its political importance at the time – at least, to the British. The war was the response of a British political initiative in South Africa, implemented by the High Commissioner, Sir Henry Bartle Frere. Known as Confederation, this policy was intended to bring the disparate and often mutually hostile groups in the region together under a loose British authority, with a long-term aim of imposing an economic development plan across the region as a whole. An advocate of Britain's Imperial vision, Frere saw no contradiction in using force to pursue such a policy; for many, the possession of empire imposed upon the British a Christian civilising mission, and for Frere and his advisers in the white settler community, the robust independence of the Zulu kingdom was incompatible with Britain's long-term aims.

However, the British government did not particularly support Frere's decision to go to war with the Zulu. Frere hoped for a quick and easy victory, a war which would be over almost before it hit the headlines; Isandlwana changed all that. Imperial pride ensured that the government in London would have to support British troops in the field, at least until military supremacy had been achieved. But in the aftermath of the war, Frere's policies were subjected to searching scrutiny, and the Confederation policy – which had led to the war in the first place – was quickly abandoned. Indeed, the battle of Isandlwana is something of a defining moment in the colonial history of South Africa, encapsulating many of the threads of European encroachment and African resistance which are common to the period as a whole. It also

perhaps typifies the futility of many of those conflicts, and the bitter legacy of the warrior traditions of either side.

For the British, the demands of empire meant that events moved swiftly on. A war to defend British India from Russian influence – the second Afghan War – which began before the invasion of Zululand, and spluttered on long after, was widely regarded at the time as being of far greater strategic and political importance, and in the end required a great British military commitment. Yet Isandlwana cast a long shadow, and it is possible to argue that had the Anglo-Zulu War never occurred, there would probably have been no war in the Transvaal in 1881, and perhaps even no Anglo-Boer War between 1899–1902. The invasion of Zululand set in motion a chain of events which had a profound long-term effect on the political geography of modern South Africa, involving not only the destruction of indigenous political systems, but the emergence of colonial rule and, ultimately, the rise of Afrikaner nationalism. Arguably, the echoes of these events have yet to fade entirely away.

For the Zulu people, of course, the war was a national calamity. As the missionary Bishop of Zululand, A.W. Lee, observed in 1949:

From the point of view of those who have experienced two world wars, with their widespread bloodshed and devastation, the story of the Zulu War of 1879 reads like that of a series of skirmishes carried on in an unimportant country for obscure reasons. Yet to the Zulu people, it was the ultimate tragedy, involving as it did the loss of independence, of self-government, and of freedom to live their lives as seemed best to them.

Chronology

1878

11 December British ultimatum delivered to Zulu representatives at Lower Thukela Drift

1879

6 January No. 4 Column (Wood) crosses river Ncome into territory claimed by the Zulu

11 January Ultimatum expires; war begins.

11 January No. 3 Column (Glyn) crosses into Zululand at Rorke's Drift

12 January No. 3 Column attacks followers of Chief Sihayo kaXongo in the Batshe valley

17 January Main Zulu army leaves oNdini (Ulundi) for the front

18 January No. 1 Column (Pearson) begins advance to Eshowe

20 January No. 4 Column establishes base at Fort Thinta

22 January Zulu attack on No. 1 Column at Nyezane river

22 January Main Zulu army attacks camp of Centre Column at Isandlwana

22/23 January Zulu attack on British border depot at Rorke's Drift

22/24 January No. 4 Column skirmishes with Zulu forces in the vicinity of the Zungwini and Hlobane mountains

23 January No. 1 Column occupies Eshowe mission

27 January First news of Isandlwana reaches No. 1 Column

28 January No. 1 Column decides to hold Eshowe

31 January No. 4 Column moves to a more secure base on Khambula hill

11 February Chelmsford's despatch regarding Isandlwana reaches London

11 February Communications between Eshowe and British bases on the Lower Thukela cut; Zulu investment of Eshowe begins

3 March First communications by signal established between Lower Thukela and Eshowe

11 March First reinforcements authorised by UK government arrive in South Africa

12 March Successful attack by Prince Mbilini's followers on convoy of 80th Regiment at Ntombe river

24 March Zulu army leaves oNdini for the northern front

28 March Unsuccessful attack by mounted men from No. 4 Column on Hlobane mountain

29 March Main Zulu army attacks No. 4 Column at Khambula, and is heavily defeated

29 March Eshowe relief column under Lord Chelmsford begins march from Thukela

1 April Prince Louis Napoleon arrives in Natal to join Lord Chelmsford's staff

2 April Chelmsford's Eshowe relief column defeats Zulu concentrations on the coast at Gingindlovu

3 April Eshowe relieved

5 April Prince Mbilini mortally wounded in a skirmish near Luneburg

11 April Last of British reinforcements arrive in Natal

13 April Chelmsford reorganises his forces into 1st Division, 2nd Division and Flying Column

20 May Significant British raid across the central Thukela (Twentyman)

21 May British Cavalry Brigade visits Isandlwana to bury some of

	the dead and carry away serviceable equipment
31 May	2nd Division crosses into Zululand
1 June	Prince Imperial killed
16 June	Chelmsford receives news that he is to be superseded by Sir Garnet Wolseley
17 June	2nd Division and Flying Column link for the final stage of the advance on oNdini
20 June	1st Division advances from bases previously established in south-eastern Zululand
25 June	Zulu raid across the central Thukela
26 June	Troops from the Flying Column destroy Zulu royal homesteads in the emaKhosini valley, the original Zulu heartland
27 June	Combined 2nd Division and Flying Column arrive at Mthonjaneni heights, above the White Mfolozi river
28 June	Sir Garnet Wolseley arrives in Durban
1 July	2nd Division and Flying Column establish camp on the White Mfolozi river, opposite oNdini
3 July	Mounted men from the Flying Column skirmish with Zulus on the Ulundi plain
4 July	Battle of Ulundi (oNdini); final defeat of the Zulu army
4/5 July	Surrenders of Zulu chiefs in coastal districts
8 July	Chelmsford resigns his command
15 July	Chelmsford hands over his command to Wolseley
19 July	Wolseley, en route to oNdini, outlines terms of surrender to Zulu chiefs in coastal districts
14 August	Wolseley accepts surrenders of royalist *amakhosi* including Mnyamana and Ntshingwayo at oNdini
28 August	Capture of King Cetshwayo by British Dragoons in the Ngome forest
4 September	King Cetshwayo taken aboard ship at Port Durnford, destined for exile in Cape Town
8 September	Last skirmishes of the war near Luneburg

The Zulu kingdom

The area now known as Zululand lies on the eastern coast of South Africa, cut off from the interior by a barrier of mountains known as the Kahlamba – or to the first white travellers as the Drakensberg, or Dragon Mountains – and from the Indian Ocean by a line of heavy surf and open beaches, broken only by the silted mouths of unnavigable rivers. The cloud-bearing winds blowing off the ocean have deposited rain for aeons in their passage across the uplands, creating powerful river systems which have cut winding passages through the corrugated hills on their way back down to the sea. Historically, before human habitation left an indelible mark on the geography, much of the area was open grassland, broken here and there by primordial forests on the ridge-tops, and by thorn-bush in the hot valley floors. The earliest human inhabitants, who survived into modern times as the San 'Bushmen', retired to the mountain foothills in the face of the inexorable advance of both black and white pastoralists, and maintained a fragile toehold until finally driven out in the middle of the 19th century. For at least 800 years the area has been home to robust African societies, while the fragmentary historical record suggests that the ancestors of the people we know today as the Zulus were in place at least as long ago as the 15th century.

At the end of the 18th century, the area of modern KwaZulu-Natal – between the Phongolo river in the north and the Umzimkhulu in the south – was populated by a large number of autonomous chiefdoms, who spoke broadly the same language, and who followed a way of life based largely on cattle. Cattle provided not only a means of sustenance – milk was a staple, and beef eaten on festive occasions – and hides for clothing and shields, but also a means of assessing wealth and status. An exchange of cattle was essential to the marriage contract, and almost every religious rite was accomplished by means of a sacrifice to the ancestral spirits. The people themselves lived in small family homesteads (*umuzi*, pl. *imizi*), each one a cluster of dome-shaped huts, made of thatch fixed over a framework of saplings and arranged around a central cattle pen, which represented home to a single family – a married man, his wives, offspring and dependent relatives. Each chiefdom was ruled over by a royal house, which produced successive generations of chiefs (*inkhosi*, pl. *amakhosi*), who dispensed authority with the assistance of a council of elders.

The wide range of grasses which characterised the region – which supported cattle throughout the year – and general fertility of the soil away from the rocky hill-tops encouraged a considerable population density, and a gradual fixing of political boundaries. In the late 18th century, however, this society was wracked by a series of conflicts of growing intensity between chiefdoms. Historians still debate the causes today, and rising population, protracted drought, and a conflict to secure dominance of the trade routes which filtered out from the Portuguese enclave at Delagoa Bay have all been convincingly argued. Quite possibly, it was a combination of all these factors, aggravating each other to various degrees. For whatever reason, in the 1790s the chiefdoms along the line of the Black and White Mfolozi rivers began to fight each other, and the old autonomous chiefdoms began to draw together to form larger, more militarily secure groupings. This process lasted for the best part of 30 years, and became increasingly violent; by the time it was over, one chiefdom had come to dominate them all – the Zulu.

The original heartland of the Zulu people lay along the banks of the Mkhumbane stream, on the middle reaches of the White

Amabutho photographed in the 1860s. It is not clear whether these are men in the Zulu king's army, or followers of a Natal *inkhosi*, but the picture nonetheless provides a rare and vivid glimpse of the appearance of Zulu regiments in their sumptuous ceremonial regalia. (MuseuMAfrica)

Mfolozi. Originally no more than a minor player in these conflicts, caught between the more powerful Ndwandwe chiefdom in the north-west, and the Mthethwa in the south-east, the Zulu rose to prominence thanks to the abilities of their young *inkhosi* Shaka kaSenzangakhona. Ambitious, dynamic and a talented military commander, King Shaka first threw off the overlordship of the Mthethwa, then in a succession of campaigns between 1817 and 1824 drove out the Ndwandwe. By the time of his death in 1824, Shaka had established a new kingdom, a conglomeration of existing groups under the rule of the Zulu elite. The core of this kingdom extended between the Black Mfolozi in the north and the Thukela in the south, while many groups in the country beyond were prepared to acknowledge Shaka's authority.

Even before Shaka died the seeds of the future conflicts had been sown. European interests in South Africa dated back to the

17th century, when the Dutch had established a way station at the extreme tip of the continent – the Cape of Good Hope – to service their ships on the long maritime haul to the Indies. In 1806 the British, as part of their global war against Napoleon and his allies, seized control of the Cape from the Dutch. The British, too, had little interest in the interior of Africa, but a momentum of settler expansion had already built up on the colonial frontiers which was difficult to contain. With the final defeat of Napoleon in 1815, the far-flung possessions of the British Empire were awash with adventurous young men made suddenly unemployed by the outbreak of peace, and this created a climate of mercantile opportunism which led directly to British involvement in Zululand. In 1824 a group of British and Dutch traders, led by an ex-Royal Navy lieutenant, Francis Farewell, crossed a dangerous sandbar and established a settlement on the edge of a lagoon which they grandly named Port Natal. Port Natal lay some 50 miles (80km) south of the main centres of Zulu settlement, but it was to King Shaka that the settlers looked for protection – and profit. To this unlikely beginning did all British claims in the area subsequently belong.

The pattern of the relationship between the Zulu kingdom and the white newcomers was established over the next 20 years. For a decade, the Port Natal community remained no more than an anarchic outpost, a frontier settlement beyond the reach of British law.

An early studio study of a white missionary and Zulus which reflects the complex relationship between colonial Natal and independent Zululand. The conflict between 19th-century concepts of 'civilisation' and 'savagery' implicit in the photograph is underscored by the Zulu girl's discreet – and untraditional – leopardskin 'dress', provided by the photographer, and by the exotic tiger-skin rug. (Ron Sheeley Collection)

Southern Africa in the 1870s

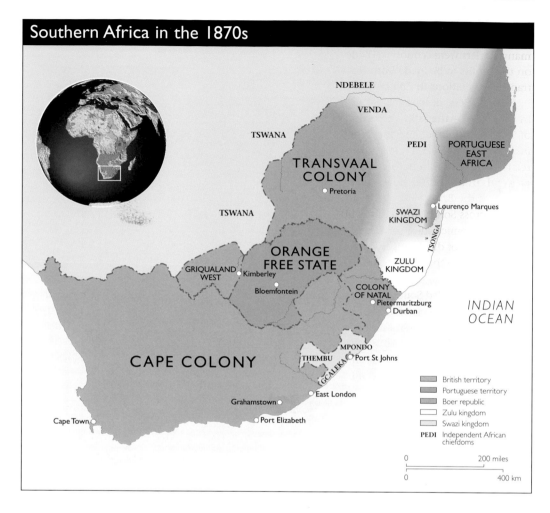

From the beginning, however, it attracted political refugees from Zululand who sought the protection of the whites, and whose presence the Zulu kings regarded as an inevitable evil. In the 1830s, however, a widespread disillusion with British authority among the Dutch-speaking settlers on the eastern Cape frontier, further south, led to a new wave of white expansion. The settlers – known to history as the Boers – crossed into KwaZulu-Natal from the interior, and were soon drawn into a bloody conflict with the Zulu over grazing land. This conflict irrevocably compromised the British group at Port Natal, who took the opportunity it afforded to break free of Zulu control. Yet the Boers could not escape the British so easily; the prospect that they might use Port Natal as a means of communicating with rival

European powers provoked an armed intervention by the Imperial authorities. Redcoats seized Port Natal in 1842, and the following year the hinterland – known as Natal – was annexed to the British Crown.

The political boundaries between Natal and the Zulu kingdom were fixed at the line of the Thukela and Mzinyathi (Buffalo) rivers, but in fact the fortunes of both were inextricably linked. Although whites exercised political power in Natal, the majority population was African, many of them groups who had resisted King Shaka, or who were political refugees from the Zulu kingdom itself. The arrival of the whites had thereby facilitated the creation of an African population on the very borders of Zululand which was generally hostile to the Zulu Royal House. The Zulu kings could no longer administer their own affairs without considering the reaction of both white and black Natal, while in turn many settlers were economically dependent on the profits to be made from hunting and trading expeditions in Zululand.

Nevertheless, despite occasional instability in both areas – the Zulu succession dispute of 1856 in Zululand, and the 'rebellion' of *inkhosi* Langalibalele in Natal in 1873 – the relationship between both parties was largely peaceful. In the 1870s, however, this was to change as the British adopted a new 'forward policy' across South Africa as a whole.

The economic motor for this policy was the discovery of diamonds in the late 1860s, in what became the boom town of Kimberley, north of the Cape. For half a century, the British had regarded South Africa as a drain on resources, a cockpit of local rivalries which demanded a high price in money and blood in return for the strategic advantages of the Cape. Yet the discovery of diamonds – and with it the tantalising promise of further

Sir Henry Bartle Edward Frere, who was sent to the Cape in 1877 as High Commissioner, to implement Britain's Confederation policy. Frere's view that the independence of the Zulu kingdom provided a threat to this policy was a direct cause of the war. (Private collection)

natural treasures to come – offered a return on the years of investment. Yet the region was sadly lacking in infrastructure of any sort, and indeed the patchwork of British colonies, Boer republics and independent African chiefdoms was a severe handicap to any attempt at developmental planning. To move labour and goods from the mines in the interior to the coastal ports would require a degree of political unity which was entirely lacking.

The solution, planned by Imperial theorists in London, was a scheme known as Confederation. In Canada – another region plagued by mutual antagonism between settler groups – an administration had been imposed, apparently successfully, which had allowed a degree of local autonomy within a framework of overall British authority. In 1877, a new British pro-consul, Sir Henry Bartle Frere, was sent out to South Africa to implement a similar scheme there.

The process had begun even before Frere arrived in Cape Town. In April, British troops had marched into Pretoria, the capital of the most northerly of the Boer territories – the South African Republic – and raised the Union Flag. The annexation of what became the Transvaal Colony was accomplished on the pretext that the Republic was both on the verge of bankruptcy, and unable to prosecute a war it had embarked upon against its African neighbours. The move took the scattered Boer community by surprise, but in due course their confusion, which the British mistook for acquiescence, would harden into an implacable opposition.

With the Transvaal, the British had inherited a long-standing dispute with the Zulu kingdom. The three territories came together in a long slice of rugged country along the eastern slopes of the northern Kahlamba mountains, a sparsely populated area which was a long way from the centres of British, Boer or Zulu authority. In the 1840s, the then Zulu king, Mpande kaSenzangakhona, had allowed republican Boers, trekking inland to escape the arrival of British authority in Natal, to graze their cattle there. Lying as it did across the headwaters of several rivers – and with no natural boundary to serve as a border – the Boers had infiltrated this territory, pressing further and further into territory claimed by the Zulu. By the 1860s, many in Zululand, led by the king's son, Prince Cetshwayo, bitterly opposed any further Boer encroachment. In 1872 King Mpande died, and the following year Cetshwayo succeeded him. A more vigorous man than his father, King Cetshwayo put pressure on the Boers to retreat from the disputed territory. For the most part, colonial officials in Natal, keen to minimise Boer influence in the region, had supported the Zulu claims. When, in 1877, those Boer farmers became British subjects, however, the British position changed. This apparent *volte face* caused considerable bitterness in Zululand, and was regarded by many Zulus as the first true step on the road to war.

In the light of this, Frere began to see the Zulu kingdom as a hindrance to the successful imposition of the Confederation scheme. Frere had brought to South Africa a global Imperial perspective, and he was

A typical frontier farm-house on the Zulu borders. The encroachment of Boer settlers along the north-western marches of the kingdom was widely resented in Zululand. (Private collection)

deeply concerned that the divided state of the region left it vulnerable to the attack of a rival empire. By the 1870s, the Zulu were by far the most powerful African group remaining in the region, where a century of colonial expansion had seen most other indigenous groups broken, reduced or dispossessed. In 1877, a wave of unrest spread through the African communities, regardless of colonial boundaries, a common reaction against the reduced circumstances in which they found themselves. In the last sad struggles of the amaXhosa, the southern Sotho and the Pedi, however, Frere saw a conspiracy to turn back the tide of history and drive out the white man, and his advisers among the settler community were quick to point an accusatory finger at the Zulu. For Frere, the Zulu were in any case an anachronism who must give way in the face of European concepts of progress.

By embarking upon a war with the Zulu, Frere reasoned, he could solve a number of problems at a stroke. He could ease the pressure on the Transvaal border, and at the same time offer the Boer community a demonstration of the advantages of British rule. He could also deliver a stern lesson to any African groups still inclined to resist by

revealing their military helplessness. And, by marching his victorious army straight from Zululand to Pretoria, he could intimidate the growing republican sentiment in the Transvaal. In the long term, the destruction of the Zulu Royal House had the added advantage that it made it much easier for Natal to manage its African population in a way which suited the interests of white settlers.

In adopting this approach, Frere acted largely without the support of the British government in London. The Colonial Office fully understood that the Confederation policy could only be implemented with an implied threat of force, but the government hoped that it could be kept to a minimum. This was not entirely a humanitarian consideration; with a fresh crisis looming on the Afghan borders, the British were reluctant to embark on a costly and bloody war at the same time in Africa. Frere – who had bombarded his superiors with a series of despatches characterising King Cetshwayo's administration as tyrannical and hostile – was nonetheless instructed to deal with the Zulu question in a spirit of forbearance.

That was not, however, his intention. Despite the fact that colonial reports estimated that King Cetshwayo had nominal control of an army of 40,000 men, while the British military presence in South Africa numbered only a handful of infantry battalions, scattered in garrisons or engaged in suppressing local outbreaks, Frere was confident that he could engineer a quick victory. This confidence was based largely on the disparity in weapon types, and on the apparently different degrees of discipline among the two armies; while the Zulus were primarily armed with shields, spears and antiquated trade guns, British troops carried the best weapons the industrial revolution could produce. Frere gambled on the expectation that he could defeat the Zulu before the government in London had time to object; and that hindsight would validate his decision.

He looked to the festering border dispute with the Transvaal to provide a cause. Here, however, he ran into an unexpected complication. The head of the colonial administration in Natal – the Lieutenant-Governor Sir Henry Bulwer – feared that an Anglo-Zulu War would inevitably embroil Natal, and that this would have potentially dangerous implications for the long-term relationship between the two communities. Bulwer foresaw a bitterness and hostility between Natal's African population and the Zulu which might last for generations. To head off such a tragedy, Bulwer offered Natal's services as a mediator between the Boer and Zulu claims. King Cetshwayo accepted with alacrity; Frere could hardly do otherwise.

The commission met in March 1878 at an obscure border crossing on the Mzinyathi river just south of the disputed territory, known as Rorke's Drift. For several months, it painstakingly sifted the evidence, examining both Boer and Zulu testimony; then, to Frere's irritation, it declared its findings broadly in favour of the Zulu claims.

While Frere pondered his next move, however, the Zulu played into his hands. In the middle of 1878, two wives of an important Zulu *inkhosi*, Sihayo kaXongo, who lived along the border opposite Rorke's Drift, fled across the Mzinyathi, to move in with lovers who lived on the Natal bank. This was a serious affront to the family honour of a man who enjoyed high status within Zululand, and while Sihayo refused to act – recognising, no doubt, that his position was politically sensitive – his sons waited until he had gone to the Zulu capital oNdini – which the British knew by a variation of the same word, Ulundi – to attend the king, then took the law into their own hands. They crossed the border with an armed force, arrested the women, dragged them back into Zulu territory, and there, according to Zulu law, put them to death.

Despite the fact that it was not unknown for fugitives to be pursued across the border by either side, this incident, coming at a time of heightened tension, served to give credibility to Frere's propaganda position that the Zulu were a truculent and dangerous neighbour. Moreover, just two months later, there was another incident further north, in the heart of the 'disputed territory'. Africans living on the outskirts of the small German mission community at Luneburg were raided, a number of them were killed, and their cattle taken. The raiders were not truly Zulus, but followers of an exiled Swazi prince, Mbilini waMswati, who had fled Swaziland after an unsuccessful succession dispute a decade before, and had given his allegiance to King Cetshwayo. Cetshwayo had given Mbilini lands on the Phongolo river, close to both Luneburg and the Swazi border, where Mbilini served as Cetshwayo's foot in the Swazi door. But the Phongolo was a long way from oNdini, and Mbilini, an adroit guerrilla leader, had sought to rebuild his fortunes by taking advantage of the unsettled frontier. This particular raid caused Cetshwayo to distance himself publicly from Mbilini's actions, but for Frere they were all the excuse he needed.

In December 1878 Frere asked Cetshwayo to send his envoys to hear the results of the long-awaited boundary commission. The meeting took place under a clump of wild fig trees on the Natal bank of the Thukela, at a well-known crossing point called the Lower Drift. As a show of Imperial force, a detachment of British sailors and marines lined up nearby, and a Durban photographer recorded the scene for posterity. Frere's representatives read out the commission's award, and the Zulus expressed their satisfaction at the fairness of it. Then, ominously, the subject turned to other matters. Frere's despatch complained of the tyranny of King Cetshwayo's administration – 'Have the Zulu complained?' asked one of the envoys – and demanded that both Mbilini and the sons of Sihayo be surrendered to be tried for their border violations. Furthermore, the British demanded that Cetshwayo disband the Zulu military system within 30 days; failing that, he would find himself at war with the British Empire.

Confrontation: Frere's representatives read the British ultimatum to Zulu envoys at the Lower Drift on the Thukela, 11 December 1878. (Killie Campbell Library)

Fight us in the open

The British

The two armies which were poised to confront one another across the spectacularly beautiful Zulu border country were radically different in type, organisation, outlook and weapons.

The British Army was a professional, full-time body, which at that time was one of the most experienced of any power anywhere in the world. The demands of policing an empire meant that British troops had fought, even by 1879, in widely varying terrain on almost every continent. Many senior officers had learned their trade as juniors in Britain's last great conventional war – the war against Russia in the Crimea – and had since served in colonial campaigns in India and Africa. Despite occasional – and sometimes spectacular – defeats in individual battles, the British Army had established a tradition of adaptability and resilience in the field which had meant that, since Queen Victoria had come to the throne in 1838, it had never lost a colonial campaign.

It was, nevertheless, essentially a conservative organisation, and one which reflected the broader divisions within Victorian Britain. The lower ranks were drawn from the poorest sector of society, and despite attempts to reform their lot, most were ill-educated labourers who took 'the Queen's Shilling' and enlisted for long periods of service as an escape from the destitution of unemployment. Life in the Army offered them a strict regime, but also the prospect of regular food, pay, adventure and, as the 1870s wore on, at least the hope that they might better themselves. Their officers, on the other hand, were mostly from the gentry and aristocracy, men whose social status had accustomed them to the exercise of authority. Both officers and other ranks could expect to spend long periods in overseas garrisons, but the officers could at least alleviate this with several months' annual leave. While officers and men alike were governed by the Army's own laws – Queen's Regulations – they had little in common otherwise, and lived largely in mutually exclusive self-contained worlds dominated by unwritten rules and codes of behaviour. It was against such a background that symbols of regimental pride and tradition – notably the Colours, which embodied their common duty to Queen and country, and recalled their past battle honours – served to bind them together.

The standard British tactical unit was the infantry battalion. Historically, most British regiments had been raised to consist of a single battalion, but in the middle of the 19th century a number of regiments had been given a second battalion and, in the case of Rifle regiments, a third. In theory, one battalion in such regiments was supposed to remain at home while the other served abroad, but the demands of Empire meant that at any given time more were rostered for overseas service than was ideal. Thus, both the 1st and 2nd Battalions of the 24th Regiment (2nd Warwickshires) were in South Africa in 1878, although they had come there separately from different peacetime postings, and had not served together in action before the Zulu campaign began.

Each battalion nominally consisted of 800 men – eight companies, each of 100 men – and a headquarters detachment and band. In the field, however, with the inevitable delays in replacing men whose time had expired, combined with high rates of sickness and with men on detached duty, it was not unusual for battalions to fight at a strength of 600 or less. Although there had been attempts in India to develop a practical and inconspicuous campaign uniform – khaki – troops elsewhere in the Empire still fought in

uniforms that differed little from their home ceremonial dress. Most infantry battalions wore red jackets, with coloured patches on their cuffs and sleeves denoting their regiment, and dark-blue trousers. In hot climates, they were issued with a white 'foreign service' helmet, which in South Africa was usually worn without the brass regimental badge on the front, and dulled with tea or coffee to offer a less obvious target. The standard infantry weapon was the robust and accurate single-shot Martini-Henry breech-loading rifle and bayonet; officers carried swords and revolvers. Cavalry regiments were rather smaller in size, and were still intended largely for shock action. As a result, although issued with carbines, they fought primarily with swords and lances.

British generals during the Victorian period seldom had the luxury of commanding sufficient men for the job, and at the time that Frere presented his ultimatum, there were just six infantry battalions in South Africa, with one more en route from Mauritius, just two light artillery batteries (each of six guns) and no regular cavalry. Moreover, there were just 19 transport and supply officers, with just 29 men under their command, who were responsible for keeping troops supplied across hundreds of miles of difficult terrain. Even given the prevailing optimism regarding the outcome of a Zulu campaign, this was clearly insufficient. Frere's military commander, Lieutenant General Lord Chelmsford,

A British infantry battalion lined up by companies, photographed in the Natal capital of Pietermaritzburg, possibly on the eve of the war. The regular infantry provided the heavy fire-power which underpinned Chelmsford's tactical planning, but there were too few available to him in the early stages of the invasion. (Private collection)

Lieutenant General Lord Chelmsford, the senior British commander in South Africa in 1879 – a formal portrait which suggests something of Chelmsford's confidence and standing within the Victorian military establishment. (Ron Sheeley collection)

appealed to London for reinforcements, but was sent only two further battalions and a stern reminder that they were to be used for defensive – rather than offensive – purposes.

To make up the numbers, Chelmsford turned to colonial Natal. The colonial administration maintained a small body of full-time professional quasi-military police – the Natal Mounted Police (NMP) – while a number of part-time volunteer units had been raised among settler society for its own defence. These were largely drawn from the active sons of the white farming gentry, who could ride and shoot, who contributed towards the cost of their own uniforms, but who were armed and equipped by the government. The numbers of such units were small, however – between 30 and 60 men apiece – and while they would prove invaluable as scouts, the colonial administration was not entirely happy to release them to Chelmsford's command. To bolster his mounted arm still further, Chelmsford authorised the creation of a number of mounted irregulars, full-time units raised by the Crown for a limited period of service. Many of these were raised on the Eastern Cape Frontier, from units disbanded when the war against the amaXhosa came to

an end, and their numbers were made up from among the rootless adventurers and drifters of colonial society.

Finally, Chelmsford turned to the African population of Natal for support. Many of the chiefdoms there had a long-standing antipathy towards the Zulu kingdom, and they offered a plentiful source of potentially motivated manpower. The colonial administration was reluctant to raise a levy, however, because of the traditional nervousness among the settlers of arming the black population. In the event, under pressure, Bulwer at last allowed Chelmsford to raise three infantry regiments – known as the Natal Native Contingent (NNC) – and a number of mounted troops. The opportunity afforded by the NNC was largely squandered by parsimony and suspicion, however. They were not raised until November 1878,

An officer of the Natal auxiliaries, and some of the men under his command. Thousands of Natal Africans fought with the Natal Native Contingent and associated units, but their military qualities were largely squandered. Poorly trained, often badly led and denied sufficient firearms, they were undervalued by British regulars and regarded with suspicion by the colonial authorities. (Private collection)

scarcely two months before the war was scheduled to begin, and while some chiefdoms contributed detachments to particular units, no attempt was made to organise them along African traditional lines. Instead, they were organised into battalions, given only a red headband as a uniform, and only one in 10 was issued with a firearm. The rest carried their own shields and spears. The officers were either British regular officers or volunteers, and some attempt was made to find men who understood the troops under their command, but there were far too few to go round. The white NCOs, by and large, were recruited from a pool of those rejected by the irregulars – most did not speak Zulu, and some did not speak English either.

In the event, much of the British experience in Zululand would be shaped by questions of logistics. Zululand was a rugged and difficult country with only a few traders' tracks to serve as roads, and British troops would need to carry all their food, ammunition, tents and equipment with them. This meant that the pace of their advance would be limited to that of their wheeled transport. Although there were a few mule-drawn army wagons available, these were not ideally suited to the open veld, and in any case they were too few. Lord Chelmsford's agents were therefore required

Colonial transport drivers and their African workers. Civilians such as these were employed in large numbers to provide the wagons necessary to move British supplies throughout the war; without them, the British columns could not have moved. (Private collection)

to buy or hire large numbers of civilian ox-drawn transport wagons from the settler population, often at inflated prices. The problem of managing the resultant baggage trains – of protecting them and keeping rates of mortality among the oxen within acceptable limits – would torment Chelmsford throughout the coming campaign.

The Zulu

In contrast to its British counterpart, the Zulu army was essentially a civilian militia. Before King Shaka's day, it had been traditional to gather youths of the same age together to form them into guilds in order to undergo the ceremonies which marked the onset of early manhood. During the early

Two young Zulus in full regalia. Each *ibutho* had a distinctive costume which was worn on ceremonial occasions – although much of it was discarded in the field. The shields carried by these men are personal war-shields, *amahawu*; when fighting with their units, they would have carried larger regimental patterns. (Private collection)

conflicts, before the rise of the Zulu, a number of chiefs had begun to use these formations as battlefield tactical units, and the process had been finely honed under Shaka. In the Zulu system, these guilds became an important part of the apparatus of state which bound the nation together.

The young men were called together at intervals of three or four years, and regardless of their local allegiances, were formed into units known as *amabutho* (sing. *ibutho*). This marked the onset of a period of part-time national service, from which they were only liable to be released when they took their first wives. They were answerable directly to the king, and by taking control of the young men – the most coercive element in African society – out of the hands of the regional chiefs, successive Zulu kings greatly reduced the risk of internal dissent. The young cadets were assembled under state officials (*induna*, pl. *izinduna*) at royal homesteads where they underwent a period of training. These homesteads, known as *amakhanda* (sing. *ikhanda*) – literally 'heads', meaning centres of royal authority – were sited strategically around the kingdom. Most consisted of two or three hundred huts, but the largest of them, where the king chose to reside, often numbered over 1,000 huts. Once they were trained, the men of the new *ibutho* would be given a regimental name and a ceremonial uniform of feathers and furs. A herd of royal cattle, matched according to the colour of the hides, would be given into their keeping, and from these they would be allowed to make war-shields. Such shields were the property of the state rather than the individual, and were kept in the *amakhanda* and issued to the regiment when it assembled.

A new regiment would either be allowed to build a new *ikhanda* to serve as its own headquarters, or be attached to that of an existing one whose members were growing old. The numbers in each *ibutho* varied according to the rate of population increase, but each one was organised into two wings, and further sub-divided into companies. The king himself appointed the officers to

command at the senior levels, but junior officers were selected from among the ranks. The duties of the *amabutho* were varied; they served not only as the king's soldiers, but as the national police force and the state labour gang, herding the king's cattle and building his huts, or taking part in national hunts. The great ceremonies which blessed the new harvest each year could only be properly completed with a muster of the entire army in ceremonial regalia.

Yet the young men only spent part of their time assembled as regiments. To keep them in their barracks and fed required a huge effort, and the barracks were empty for most of the year, watched over by a caretaker staff. The men lived among their families, and were perhaps called up for only three or four months of the year, whenever the king had need of their services.

This commitment lasted until the men married – an important rite of passage within Zulu society which marked the onset of full adult status. As a result, the Zulu kings had taken to themselves the right to allow men to marry, and permission was usually given to groups as a whole. To maintain the young men at their disposal, it was traditional for the kings to refuse to allow the *amabutho* to marry until the members were at least in their 30s. This was an aspect of Zulu life which both shocked and titillated the British, but in fact Zulu moral codes connived at limited sexual activity outside marriage, and Frere's famous description of the Zulu as 'celibate man-destroying gladiators' is deeply misleading. Once a regiment was given permission to marry, the men dispersed, took wives, and marked their new status with a polished ring of gum bound into their hair. They still acknowledged their allegiance to their *amabutho*, but married regiments were regarded as a national reserve, which was only called out in times of emergency.

Since King Shaka's time, the Zulu had been primarily armed with a long-bladed stabbing spear, which was designed to be used at close quarters. As a result they had perfected an aggressive battlefield tactic designed to bring their men to contact as quickly and efficiently as possible. Known as *izimpondo zankomo*, 'the beasts' horns', this was an encircling movement in which flanking parties, the 'horns', surrounded an enemy, and pinned him in place for the assault of the central body, the 'chest'. Although designed for use against African enemies, this tactic remained in use against European opponents as well until long after the Anglo-Zulu War. Throwing spears – discouraged in Shaka's reign – had been reintroduced in the 1830s to offer a minimal response to musketry, and by the 1870s the Zulu army also possessed large numbers of firearms, imported into the country by white traders. Some British reports suggested that there were as many as 20,000 guns in

Zululand on the eve of war. Although these included a scattering of comparatively recent models, most by far were long obsolete by British standards, and their accuracy was not improved by poor-quality powder and home-made bullets.

On the march, the Zulu army was perfectly at home in its natural environment, and could easily cross obstacles which would confound their British counterparts. Although the speed at which an army could march has been prone to exaggeration, they could easily cover 20 miles (32km) a day for days at a time. They lived off cattle which they drove with them, and when these were exhausted they foraged among the communities through which they moved. Their advance was screened by scouts who were thrown out many miles in advance of the main army, and when operating on home ground, they were fed with intelligence by the civilian population.

As a result, throughout the 1879 campaign, the Zulus were almost always aware of the conspicuous movements of their enemy, while the British seldom discovered Zulu movements until they were attacked.

A Zulu married man and his wife. Marriage was an important rite of passage within Zulu society, and this was reflected within the military system. Married men were distinguished by a ring of fibre and gum worn on their heads – visible here – and were no longer required to meet the full obligations of national service. (Private collection)

British invasion plans

As he had planned that it should, Frere's ultimatum presented King Cetshwayo with an impossible dilemma. The king and his councillors recognised the extreme danger of a war with the British, but were divided on how best to respond. They were prepared to make concessions to the British demands, but they could hardly allow themselves to be dictated to over the issue of the army. All attempts at negotiation were rebuffed – and on 11 January 1879 the Anglo-Zulu War began.

Frere's political initiative required that Chelmsford mount an offensive campaign. Fresh from the closing stages of the Cape Frontier War – where the amaXhosa had largely refused to be drawn into open battle – Chelmsford was preoccupied by the fear that the Zulu army might be reluctant to fight. Frere needed the war to be short and successful, and in any case a protracted campaign would add immeasurably to Chelmsford's logistical problems. Convinced of the superiority of British training and firepower, he had no doubts that he would win any direct confrontation, and his strategy was shaped by the need to pin the Zulu down. Ironically, Chelmsford failed to appreciate that for the Zulu, too, a quick and decisive campaign was also highly desirable, to release the men of the *amabutho* to their civilian responsibilities.

King Cetshwayo's capital was a cluster of royal homesteads surrounding his favourite *ikhanda*, oNdini, in the heart of the country, just north of the White Mfolozi river. Lord Chelmsford made this his objective. Initially, Chelmsford intended to advance from five separate points along the Natal and Transvaal borders, following tracks where they existed, and converging on oNdini. Moreover, diplomatic efforts were made to induce the Swazi kingdom, to the north, to enter the war on Britain's side, to ensure that the Zulu were largely surrounded. In the event, however, the Swazi refused to commit themselves, and the difficulty of assembling sufficient transport vehicles meant that Chelmsford had to reduce his offensive columns to three, keeping the other two smaller columns in reserve. The offensive columns were placed to cross into Zululand at the Lower Drift on the Thukela, in the east of the country, at Rorke's Drift along the middle border, and at the Transvaal border village of Utrecht, in the disputed territory. Each offensive column consisted of a core of British regulars – two battalions of infantry, and an artillery battery – a unit of African auxiliaries, and a number of volunteer or irregular cavalry units. The reserve columns were smaller; one, consisting almost entirely of auxiliary troops, was placed at Middle Drift on the Thukela – between the Lower and Rorke's Drifts – while the other was assembled further north, beyond Luneburg, at a spot where the Zulu, Swazi and Transvaal borders converged.

As the columns assembled in late 1878, the weather turned against them. For several years the region had been in the grip of a drought, and to the discomfort of men living under canvas, at last it broke. The high temperatures of the Zululand summer would be interspersed with frequent heavy downpours, which flooded the rivers and turned the tracks to mud.

In the event, the British began their advance prematurely – troops from the left flank column, under Colonel Wood, crossed the Ncome river into Zulu territory a few days before the ultimatum expired. On the 11th, the remaining columns crossed the border – and the war began in earnest.

The Zulu did not contest the crossing. Many civilians had abandoned the border areas, driving their cattle away to natural strongholds, but while some warriors stayed

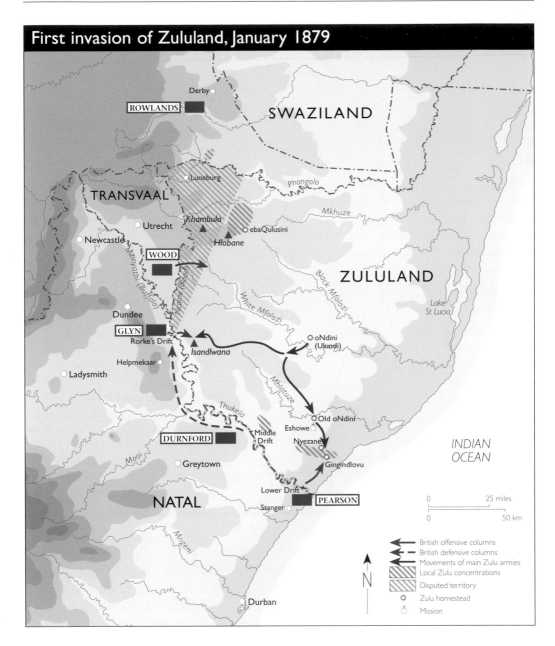

First invasion of Zululand, January 1879

to watch British movements, King Cetshwayo had already summoned the *amabutho* to oNdini. Here they underwent the ceremonies necessary to prepare them for war. Although he had some 40,000 troops nominally at his disposal, the king realised that these were insufficient to make a determined response on all three fronts, and together with his generals he decided to wait to see how the British plan unfolded. His scouts watched the British movements carefully; only once the British had committed themselves did the Zulu deploy to oppose them.

The January battles

The central British thrust, advancing from Rorke's Drift, was under the command of Colonel Richard Glyn of the 24th. Lord Chelmsford expected that this column would bear the brunt of the fighting, however, and for this reason he decided to accompany it in person – a move which largely deprived Glyn of a meaningful role. In the days ahead, it would be Chelmsford's decisions which shaped the unfolding events.

Directly ahead of Chelmsford on the Rorke's Drift line, just a few miles beyond the border, lay the territory of *inkhosi* Sihayo, whose sons had committed the border violation cited in Frere's ultimatum.

Colonel Henry Evelyn Wood, who commanded the British left flank (No. 4) column. Wood was an aggressive and occasionally reckless commander with a flair for colonial warfare, and the fighting in the northern theatre developed a distinctive character of its own. (Ron Sheeley collection)

Chelmsford felt a need to make a strong beginning to the campaign, and the proximity of Sihayo's homesteads allowed him to maintain the fiction that the war was essentially a punitive one. On 12 January, Chelmsford made a foray from his camp on the Zulu bank to attack Sihayo's followers. Neither the *inkhosi* himself nor his senior sons were at home – they were at oNdini with the general muster – but a number of Sihayo's warriors made a stand among the boulders at the foot of a line of cliffs near his homestead. Chelmsford sent his auxiliaries to attack, and supported them with the 24th, and after a sharp fight the Zulus broke and fled. Some 60 Zulus were killed, including one of Sihayo's sons, and troops set fire to the *inkhosi*'s homestead.

Chelmsford was pleased with the results of this, the first encounter of the war. Although he noted that the Zulus had fought bravely, he nonetheless felt that they were unequal to his own command – a reaction which reinforced a dangerous and widespread sense of complacency within the British camp.

In fact, it was news of the attack on Sihayo's followers which finally decided the Zulu strategy. Recognising that the British centre column seemed to be the most dangerous and aggressive of the three, the king decided to despatch his main army to attack it. In order to prevent the flanking columns from offering support, however, Zulus living in the northern and south-eastern sectors of the country were ordered to harass the British advances there as best they could. The king did not command the army in person, confining himself to offering advice, and giving actual command to his most trusted general, *inkhosi* Ntshingwayo kaMahole. The great army, upwards of 25,000 strong, left the oNdini

No photographic likeness of the senior Zulu general, Ntshingwayo kaMahole, has ever been authenticated; this photograph is widely held to be him, however, and conforms to written descriptions. The victor of Isandlwana, he was killed in 1883 during the Zulu civil war. (MuseuMAfrica)

area on 17 January, and after parading before the graves of the king's ancestors to secure their blessing, moved up to the heights west of the White Mfolozi. Here it divided, the main portion moving westwards under Ntshingwayo and Mavumengwana kaNdlela, while a force of 3,500 warriors under Godide kaNdlela – Mavumengwana's brother – peeled off and turned south, to reinforce the men in the coastal sector.

Ironically, circumstances contrived to force the Zulu to fight on all three fronts on the same day – 22 January – despite the fact that it was the day of the new moon, a time of ill-omen. Across the country, this response largely caught the British invaders by surprise.

The fighting began in the north. Here, Wood's left flank column had established a base at Fort Thinta, on the headwaters of the White Mfolozi. From the first, Wood had recognised that his war would be more fluid in character than elsewhere in the country, because the local Zulu groups enjoyed a good deal of autonomy, but were at the same time fiercely committed to the Zulu cause. Rather than the pitched battle against the royal army anticipated by Chelmsford, Wood

expected to wage a running fight against local elements. In particular, he was worried about two groups north of him – the abaQulusi, and their ally Prince Mbilini. The abaQulusi were descendents of the inhabitants of an *ikhanda* founded in the region by King Shaka, who had settled the area and come to dominate it. They regarded themselves as a sector of the Royal House itself, and they operated from a chain of mountain plateaux which served as strongholds. Prince Mbilini lived further north, near Luneburg, and while he commanded only a few hundred retainers, he was already an experienced guerrilla leader.

On the 22nd, while Mbilini was conferring with abaQulusi leaders, Wood struck north from Fort Thinta, intending to capture Zungweni mountain, the nearest of the abaQulusi strongholds. His move caught the Zulu by surprise, and after a running

dawn. Shortly before leaving the camp, he gave orders for one of the reserve columns, originally placed at Middle Drift, to march to Isandlwana.

Chelmsford left five companies of the 1/24th and one of the 2/24th in the camp, together with two guns and a number of auxiliaries and Volunteers. They were under the command of a reliable administrator, Lieutenant Colonel Henry Pulleine of the 1/24th. By the time the support column, commanded by Colonel Anthony Durnford, arrived, there were 1,700 men in the camp.

Early in the morning, a body of several hundred Zulu had appeared on the crest of a ridge overlooking the camp a mile or two to the left. They had retired before Durnford arrived, but in the absence of any instructions from Chelmsford to the contrary, Durnford decided to take his own command to investigate their movements. Splitting his men into two, he swept across and below the high ground. About 5 miles (8km) from the camp, one of Durnford's detachments pursued some Zulu scouts over a rocky rise – and found themselves looking into the faces of 25,000 Zulus, resting in the valley of the Ngwebeni stream below.

Chelmsford's intelligence reports had been largely correct. The main army had approached Isandlwana from the east, masking its approach behind the same line of hills above the Mangeni where Dartnell had made contact. Instead of moving south, however, as Chelmsford had anticipated, they had moved north, and occupied the valley undetected. They had intended to lie quiet on the 22nd, but no sooner were they discovered than they rose up in confusion out of the valley. The attack was a spontaneous one, and the Zulu generals were able to restrain only those *amabutho* camped furthest from the British incursion, and form them into a reserve.

The Zulu attack spilled out over the heights, driving back Durnford's scattered detachments. In the camp, Pulleine reacted to news of the encounter by deploying his guns and infantry in a screen to the north, making use of the *dongas* (erosion gulleys) which

The battlefield of Isandlwana today, photographed from the air. The British camp was along the foot of the mountain (left), and the British firing line was initially drawn up on the open ground (centre). The Zulu 'chest' attack was from the right. (Private collection)

drained off the hills as a defensive feature. Neither he nor his officers appreciated the extent of the danger, however, until the Zulu centre began to spill over the skyline. Durnford himself took up a position in a *donga* on the extreme right of Pulleine's line. This compelled Pulleine to extend his troops still further, until at last the line became unsustainable. Durnford abandoned the *donga* and fell back on the camp, and when Pulleine attempted to withdraw his infantry companies in response to this, the Zulu mounted a determined assault, and the British position collapsed. The Zulu centre pushed the British back through the camp and into the valley of the Manzimnyama stream beyond, which had already been occupied by the right horn. Fierce British resistance prevented the two horns from completing the encirclement, but although a number of auxiliaries managed to escape, the infantry were largely destroyed. The Zulu pursued the survivors across country as far as the Mzinyathi river.

Over 1,300 British, colonial and auxiliary troops were killed at Isandlwana. Most of the survivors were auxiliaries; both Durnford and Pulleine were among the dead. The entire camp – and with it nearly 1,000 Martini-Henry rifles – was captured by the Zulu. Yet, despite the comprehensive nature of their victory, the Zulu losses were also severe. Over 1,000 men were killed outright, their bodies buried by their comrades in *dongas*, grain-pits of nearby homesteads, or simply covered over with their shields, while perhaps as many again suffered wounds which were beyond the skills of their herbalists to cure.

Rorke's Drift

When the Zulu army rushed out of the Ngwebeni valley, *inkhosi* Ntshingwayo had been able to restrain only those *amabutho* who were camped furthest from the British incursion. These were middle-aged married men of the uThulwana, iNdlondlo, uDloko and iNdluyengwe regiments, who were quartered at the royal homestead of oNdini itself. Led by one of the most able Zulu

commanders of the age, *inkhosi* Zibhebhu kaMapitha, these regiments swung wide of the attack, cutting the road between Isandlwana and the crossing at Rorke's Drift. Some elements were despatched to harry British survivors at the river, but most continued across country until they reached the Mzinyathi. During the pursuit, however, Zibhebhu had been wounded in the hand, and retired from the field. Command passed to the king's younger brother, Prince Dabulamanzi kaMpande. Shrewd, aggressive and reckless, Dabulamanzi felt that his men had missed much of the glory of the great victory. King Cetshwayo had instructed his warriors not to cross into British territory – he wanted to be able to claim, in any subsequent peace negotiations, that he had fought only in self-defence – and indeed most of those who had followed the running fight from the camp were content to abandon it at the border. Prince Dabulamanzi, however, led his men across the river below Rorke's Drift, and into Natal.

The Zulu attack at Rorke's Drift was in no sense a planned invasion, but rather an opportunist raid in the aftermath of a spectacular victory. A long stretch of the border lay open, and once they were in British territory, some of Dabulamanzi's warriors dispersed to loot abandoned African homesteads along the river. The majority, however, headed upstream towards the mission post at Rorke's Drift.

The post at Rorke's Drift consisted of two thatched single-storey buildings, built by a trader named James Rorke 30 years before, and recently taken over by the Swedish mission society. Chelmsford had requisitioned them as a hospital and commissariat depot, where supplies were stockpiled before being sent forward to the column. On 22 January, the post was guarded by a single company of the 2/24th – B Company, under Lieutenant Bromhead – and a detachment of NNC. There were a number of medical personnel caring for sick soldiers in the makeshift hospital building, and a handful of commissaries, all under the command of the senior ranking officer, Lieutenant John Chard of the Royal

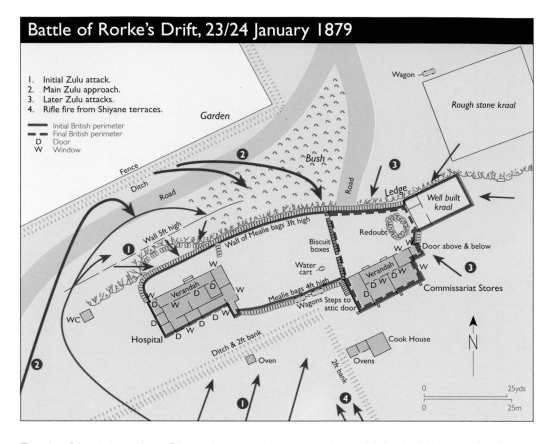

Battle of Rorke's Drift, 23/24 January 1879

1. Initial Zulu attack.
2. Main Zulu approach.
3. Later Zulu attacks.
4. Rifle fire from Shiyane terraces.

— Initial British perimeter
- - Final British perimeter
D   Door
W   Window

Garden

Bush

Wagon

Rough stone kraal

Fence

Ditch

Road

Ledge

Well built kraal

Wall 5ft high

Wall of Mealie bags 3ft high

Redoubt

Biscuit boxes

Door above & below

Water cart

Verandah

Commissariat Stores

Verandah

Mealie bags 4ft high

Wagons   Steps to attic door

WC

Hospital

Ditch & 2ft bank

2ft bank

Oven

Ovens

Cook House

N

0   25yds
0   25m

The ruins of the mission station at Eshowe, photographed at the end of the war. The picture shows the interior of Pearson's fort, including the old mission bell; much of the post was destroyed during the British evacuation, the process then being completed by the Zulu. (Private collection)

Battle of Isandlwana, 22 January 1879

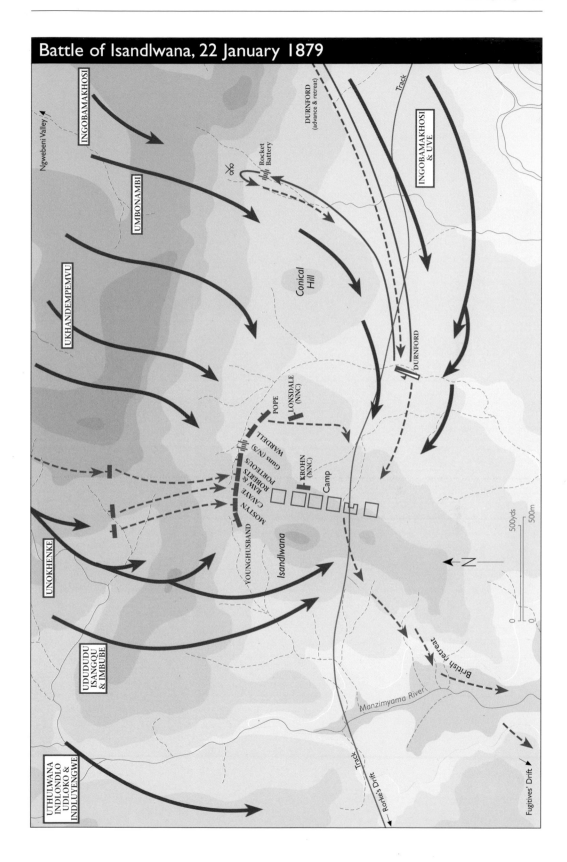

Ngwebeni Valley

INGOBAMAKHOSI

UMBONAMBI

UKHANDEMPEMVU

UNOKHENKE

UDUDUDU
ISANGQU
& IMBUBE

UTHULWANA
INDLONDLO
UDLOKO &
INDLUTENGWE

DURNFORD
(advance & retreat)

Track

INGOBAMAKHOSI
& UVE

Rocket
Battery

Conical
Hill

DURNFORD

LONSDALE
(NNC)

POPE

WARDELL

Guns (N/S)

PORTEOUS

ROBERTS

RAW &
CAVAYE

MOSTYN

YOUNGHUSBAND

KROHN
(NNC)

Camp

Isandlwana

British retreat

Manzimyama River

Track

Rorke's Drift

Fugitives' Drift

N

500yds
500m

Prince Dabulamanzi kaMpande, who led the Zulu attack on Rorke's Drift. He later retired to his home in the coastal sector, and supervised much of the siege of Eshowe; he commanded the Zulu right 'horn' at Gingindlovu, where he received a flesh-wound in the leg. (Pietermaritzburg Archives Depot)

Engineers, who had been in charge of the flat-bottomed ferry at the drift itself. When news of the disaster at Isandlwana reached the garrison, they decided not to abandon the post, but to improvise a fort from the supplies instead, linking the two buildings with lines of mealie (corn) sacks and biscuit boxes.

The approach of the Zulu caused the NNC detachment to flee, leaving little more than 150 men to defend the post against a Zulu force in excess of 3,000. The Zulu, advancing up the river and approaching from behind the Shiyane hill, launched a series of piecemeal attacks on the post, moving round to occupy a patch of garden and cultivated land which lay only a few yards from the front of the buildings. From here, they successfully drove the British back from the barricade in front of the hospital, while riflemen, taking up a position on the slopes of Shiyane, harassed the defenders with long-range fire. At about 6.00 pm, Chard decided to abandon the yard between the two buildings, falling back to a more secure position in front of the storehouse.

This allowed the Zulu to concentrate their attacks on the hospital, and they forced a

Lt. John Chard, Royal Engineers, the senior British officer at Rorke's Drift. A particularly dashing portrait in dress uniform taken at the height of Chard's fame, shortly after his return to the UK. (Ron Sheeley Collection)

way into the building, setting fire to the roof, and driving the defenders from room to room, or to scatter and take refuge outside in the growing gloom. In an epic struggle, the defenders managed to extricate most of the patients, and carry them safely across to the storehouse lines.

By this time, it was dark, and Zulu attempts to assault the front of the British position were hampered by the light from the hospital roof, which illuminated their attacks. Instead, they shifted their attention to the far end of the post, and drove the British out of a stone cattle enclosure which abutted the storehouse. The defenders were left occupying little more than the storehouse building and the barricaded yard in front of it.

By about midnight, however, the intensity of the Zulu attacks began to wane, and the battle degenerated into a sporadic firefight which lasted until shortly before dawn. Most of the Zulu withdrew during the night, exhausted by their long march across country and by the intensity of the fighting,

Lt. Gonville Bromhead, who commanded B Company, 2/24th, at Rorke's Drift. (Ron Sheeley Collection)

and discouraged by their inability to storm the last British position. By dawn, only the rearguard was still in sight, and to the delight of the garrison, they refused to rejoin the fight.

Shortly afterwards, Lord Chelmsford's detachment returned to Rorke's Drift to reinforce the garrison. After a frustrating day in the Mangeni hills, searching in vain for the forces seen by Dartnell the night before, Chelmsford had been alerted by a number of messages to the fact that something unusual had occurred at Isandlwana. By the time he had concentrated his men, however, and returned to Isandlwana, it was dusk, and the battle was long over. With his men tired after a day's marching, and unwilling to blunder into a victorious Zulu army in the dark, Chelmsford bivouacked on the bloody field overnight, his men taking what sleep they could among the corpses strewn about. Before dawn, he marched back to Rorke's Drift, passing some elements of Prince Dabulamanzi's retreating command along the way. His delight that the post had held was tempered by the awful realisation that few from the camp had escaped to Rorke's Drift – and that the centre column had been bloodily driven out of Zululand.

Just 17 of Chard's men were killed in the battle of Rorke's Drift, a testament to their courage and endurance, and to the effectiveness of their barricades. By contrast, over 350 Zulu bodies were recovered from around the post, and as many as 250 more lay out on the line of retreat. The Zulu had paid a heavy price for their tenacity.

Aftermath

The aftermath of a single day's fighting on 22 January was devastating. Counting their losses on all three fronts together, the Zulu had lost perhaps 3,000 men, a day's toll which would not be exceeded throughout the rest of the war. Yet, whereas British losses were much lighter, Lord Chelmsford had undoubtedly suffered the greater reverse.

The battle of Rorke's Drift. The dogged courage of the garrison, and the failure of the
Zulu to storm the post in 10 hours of fighting, afforded lessons which came to
dominate the tactical thinking of both sides as the war progressed. (Private collection)

Although the stand at Rorke's Drift salvaged something of British prestige – the garrison became public heroes, and 11 of them were awarded Britain's highest award for valour, the Victoria Cross – the action itself had been of little strategic significance. The centre column had been utterly defeated; all the camp equipment, reserve ammunition and supplies were captured, and the entire column's transport was abandoned on the field. The survivors were left to huddle behind improved defensive positions at Rorke's Drift, hungry and without shelter, to await a renewed Zulu attack.

Indeed, apart from the remnants of Glyn's column and a few scattered depot garrisons, the entire border between Utrecht in the north and the Lower Thukela Drift lay open to Zulu counter-attack. Chelmsford himself rode to the colonial capital, Pietermaritzburg, to report the disaster, and as news spread settlers along the length of the border fled into protective *laagers*. Barricades were even thrown up as far away as Durban. For two or three short weeks, the military initiative was in King Cetshwayo's hands. Yet in truth, he was unable to exploit it. The battles of the 22 January had exhausted his army, which had dispersed to undergo post-combat purification rituals, and to recover, and the king in any case saw little point in carrying the war into Natal. There was little hope of overrunning major civilian or military concentrations, and Cetshwayo realised that any such victory was in any case more likely to provoke an even harsher British response. His chief objective remained to defend his country, and to hope that by prolonging the war British political resolve would collapse.

The repercussions of the defeat at Isandlwana were most immediately felt by the flanking columns. In the dark days after the disaster, Chelmsford baldly informed their commanders that they were

In the aftermath of the Zulu victory at Isandlwana, the settler community in Natal was seized with widespread panic. This photograph shows precautions for defence at Greytown, on the road from Pietermaritzburg to Rorke's Drift. The conspicuous military tents are protected by trip-wires spread between the wooden stakes, foreground, and by broken bottles – both designed to impede the approach of the bare-footed Zulu. (Private collection)

unsupported, could expect to be attacked at any time, and should act as they saw fit. In the north, Colonel Wood reacted by moving his camp to a more defensible position along a long, open ridge known as Khambula. From here, he determined to keep up pressure on local Zulu groups, and once he felt secure he resumed his programme of raiding.

For Colonel Pearson's coastal column, however, the situation was more problematic. Although the Eshowe mission could be turned into a defensible post, it was 30 miles (48km) from the border, and the lines of communication were conspicuously vulnerable. Clearly, it was impractical to advance further, but at the same time any retreat would be deeply discouraging to the British cause. Pearson resolved to dig in, and await developments. A rampart was thrown up around the post, and in time Eshowe was turned into the most sophisticated fieldwork the British built during their time in Zululand. It was impossible to protect and provision the entire garrison, however, and most of Pearson's volunteer cavalry and NNC auxiliaries were sent back to the border. Within days of their passing, the Zulu cut the road and Pearson and 1,700 of his men found themselves under siege.

In the meantime, Chelmsford's despatch to the British government had reached London. Although shocked to find that Frere had committed them to a war – and one, moreover, which had begun so badly – the Disraeli administration felt it imperative that British prestige be restored as quickly as possible. To abandon the campaign would produce exactly the opposite reaction to the one Frere had intended: the frailty of the British hold over South Africa would be woefully exposed, and both African groups and the republican element in the Transvaal could be expected to take advantage of the British collapse. Ironically, by his victory at Isandlwana, King Cetshwayo had set in motion a train of events which would lead to his ultimate defeat. British reinforcements were hurried to South Africa.

The British recovery

Although a few scattered British detachments were hurried to Natal from around the Empire, the first of the reinforcements sent from the UK were unlikely to arrive before the middle of March. In the meantime, Lord Chelmsford could do little beyond encourage his remaining commanders along the border to hold on.

On the coastal front, Pearson's column was surrounded by the Zulu. Cetshwayo and his advisers had learned the lesson of Rorke's Drift, however, and the king had forbidden his army to mount further attacks on barricaded positions. He was nevertheless indignant that Pearson had set up camp in the heart of Zululand, as if the British already owned the country, and he had directed his commanders to try to lure the British into the open. Hundreds of warriors living in the coastal districts assembled at the royal homesteads near Eshowe, and from here they established a screen around the post, watching British movements and harassing them if they strayed too far from the fort. British patrols were fired upon, cavalry vedettes were ambushed, and guards mounted to protect British transport animals were sniped at.

Pearson, however, refused to be drawn out. By day, troops were allowed to move about near the camp if there was no obvious risk, but at night they slept within the walls. There was no room in the interior for tents, and most of the men slept under wagons or on the open ground. The weather remained temperamental, and the nightly downpours soon turned the interior of the fort into a quagmire. After several weeks, rations became at first monotonous, and then in short supply, and despite vigorous attempts to keep to strict sanitary arrangements, the men's health began to suffer. The toll from dysentery and typhus began to rise.

More dangerous than Zulu action, however, was the sense of *ennui* which resulted from the garrison's isolation from the course of the wider war. When Lord Chelmsford began the invasion, there was

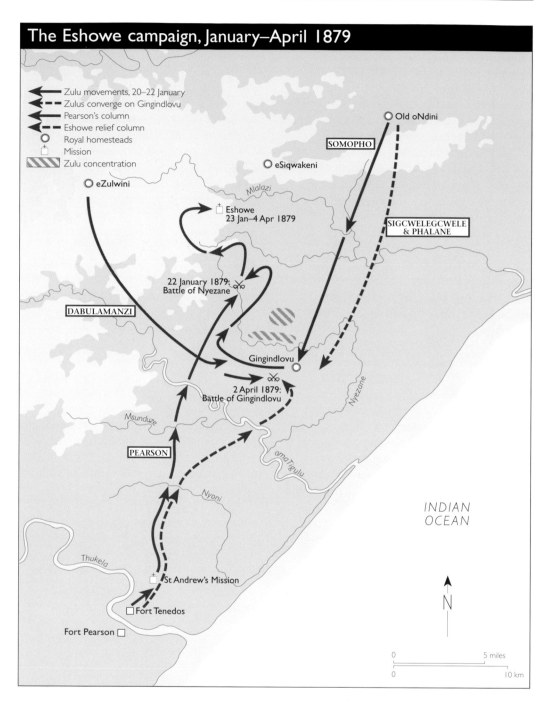

The Eshowe campaign, January–April 1879

Zulu movements, 20–22 January
Zulus converge on Gingindlovu
Pearson's column
Eshowe relief column
○ Royal homesteads
✝ Mission
▨ Zulu concentration

○ eZulwini

○ eSiqwakeni

○ Old oNdini

SOMOPHO

Mlalazi

✝ Eshowe
23 Jan–4 Apr 1879

SIGCWELEGCWELE
& PHALANE

22 January 1879:
Battle of Nyezane

DABULAMANZI

Gingindlovu

2 April 1879:
Battle of Gingindlovu

Nyezane

Msunduze

PEARSON

amaTigulu

INDIAN
OCEAN

Nyoni

Thukela

✝ St Andrew's Mission

□ Fort Tenedos

Fort Pearson □

N

0   5 miles
0   10 km

no heliograph equipment in Natal, so that once the Zulu had cut the road to the Thukela, Pearson had no means at all of communicating with the garrison left at the Lower Drift – despite the fact that it was dimly visible from the hills around the fort – nor they with him. For several weeks,

Pearson's Engineers struggled with remarkable ingenuity to improvise some means of signalling, experimenting with hot-air balloons, and large rotating screens of paper. None were successful. In the end, however, at the beginning of March the Thukela garrison managed to improvise a heliograph with the aid of a mirror from a settler's inn nearby, and, their ingenuity stimulated by the distant twinkling, the Eshowe garrison responded with something similar, made from an officer's shaving mirror and a length of pipe from the mission roof. Although both sides were dependent upon good weather, Pearson was at least able to reassure Natal that his garrison still held out, while in return Chelmsford assured him that he was assembling forces for his relief.

It was on the northern front, however, that the war first moved into a new active phase. Here, Wood had kept up pressure on the abaQulusi by raiding their homesteads and looting their cattle – a use of 'the big stick' which was balanced with the alluring appeal of a carrot. Recognising the semi-independent nature of the local *amakhosi*, Wood at the same time attempted to persuade local groups to abandon their allegiance to King Cetshwayo, offering them safety for their adherents and cattle, and protection against reprisals. For the most part he met with only limited success, but in early March he achieved a major political coup. Prince Hamu kaNzibe was a powerful member of the Zulu Royal House who lived to the north-east of Khambula, beyond abaQulusi territory.

Although he was biologically a son of King Mpande – and therefore Cetshwayo's brother – the complex Zulu laws of genealogy meant that Hamu was actually considered an heir to Mpande's brother, Nzibe. This had debarred him from any claim to succeed Mpande, but Hamu's relationship with Cetshwayo was always problematic. He was widely rumoured to resent Cetshwayo's ascendancy, and had quarrelled with the king over the course of the war. Before hostilities began, Hamu had entered into secret negotiations with Wood, but he was wary of openly defecting for fear of the reaction of abaQulusi loyalists, who lay between his territory and the sanctuary of the British. In the first week of March, however, Hamu finally fled to the Swazi border and from there made his way to Khambula, and over the next few days British troops escorted in hundreds of his followers.

Prince Hamu's defection was enormously encouraging to the British, who hoped that it was the beginning of a wholesale break-up

A group of Swazi warriors photographed in a British camp on the northern front. The British hoped to persuade the Swazi to join them in their war against the Zulu, but the Swazi remained uncommitted until the very last days of the war. (Private collection)

of the Zulu kingdom. It also, moreover, offered the British a useful addition to their manpower, as many of Hamu's warriors – most of whom had fought with the king's *amabutho* at Isandlwana – were drafted into Wood's auxiliary units.

But if Wood thought that Hamu's surrender would discourage support for the war among the Zulu in the north, Prince Mbilini would prove him decidedly wrong, for within days of Hamu's surrender, he dealt British prestige in the area a heavy and unexpected blow. A British outpost had been established at the village of Luneburg, which lay north of Khambula, and halfway to the reserve force commanded by Colonel Rowlands on the Swazi border. Luneburg was considered particularly vulnerable because of Mbilini's stronghold nearby, and the Prince regularly raided surrounding African settlements. His raids before the war had been cited in Frere's ultimatum; indeed, on 11 February Mbilini had made another such raid, targeting the farms of black Christian converts, killing a number of men, women and children and carrying away their cattle. To protect the settlement and the outlying areas, five companies of the 80th Regiment, originally part of Rowlands' column, were marched to Luneburg to protect it.

These companies were supplied by means of an extended line which began in the Transvaal and passed through the hamlet of Derby to the north. For the first part of this journey, no escort was considered necessary, but between Derby and Luneburg it was recognised that a Zulu attack was possible. At the end of February a company from the Luneburg garrison was sent to Derby to meet a convoy of 18 supply and ammunition wagons and bring them in safely. The weather was atrocious, and in the constant rain the wagons became bogged down in the mud and separated. Urged by the commander of the Luneburg garrison to march to the settlement as quickly as possible, the escort promptly abandoned the wagons on the road. To rectify this, on 7 March, a company-sized detachment of the 80th under Captain David Moriarty was sent out to gather them in. The

first wagons had reached the Ntombe river, just a few miles from Luneburg, but the river had risen, and the drivers had not been able to get the wagons across. The rest of the convoy was scattered down several miles of road beyond. Moriarty collected the wagons together and, improvising a raft, managed to ferry two to the other side, but the water level fluctuated dramatically, and the rest were stranded on the far bank. The rain scarcely ceased for several days, and Moriarty's men were wet and demoralised. Moreover, the proximity of the comparative safety at Luneburg had made Moriarty careless, and the wagons were not formed into an effective defensive arrangement.

The night of 11/12 March was once again wet, and a heavy mist rose off the river. Moriarty was sleeping on the far bank, with 70 of his men, while Lieutenant Harward commanded a detachment of 34 men on the Luneburg side. A distant shot during the night alerted some of the men, but Moriarty dismissed the report, and ordered the men back to sleep. Then, shortly before dawn, a sentry on the north bank saw a body of several hundred Zulu just 50 yards away, and approaching rapidly through the mist. The target had been too tempting to miss; Prince Mbilini had assembled more than 800 men, drawn from his own followers, the abaQulusi, and Zulu from the king's regiments whose homes lay nearby. They struck Moriarty's camp before the soldiers could form up to stop them. On the north bank, most of the men were killed as they rushed out of their tents. On the south bank, the commotion gave Harward's party a few moments' warning, and a detachment under Sergeant Booth put up a stiff defence. As the Zulus began to cross the river in large numbers, Harward's position collapsed, however, and while Sergeant Booth and a knot of men began a fighting retreat, Harward rode off towards Luneburg to raise the alarm.

By the time he returned with part of the Luneburg garrison, the Zulu had ransacked the camp and retired. Nearly 80 British troops and civilian wagon drivers were killed, among them Moriarty himself, and the Zulu

Prince Mbilini waMswati, (right). Prince Mbilini was a disaffected member of the Swazi Royal House, who had given allegiance to King Cetshwayo, and had settled on the upper Phongolo. He proved to be the most talented guerrilla leader of the war, harassing British movements between Khambula and Luneburg, and playing a decisive role in the battles of Ntombe and Hlobane. (Killie Campbell Library).

Prince Mbilini's successful attack on the stranded convoy
of the 80th Regiment at the Ntombe drift, 12 March. The
battle was the most spectacular of Mbilini's guerrilla
successes in the northern sector. (Private collection)

had carried off the transport oxen, rifles,
ammunition and some of the supplies.
Some 30 Zulu bodies were found scattered
about – a small price to pay for such a
spectacular victory. With Moriarty dead,
praise and blame were apportioned among
the living; Booth was awarded the VC for his
gallantry, while Harward was court-
martialled for deserting his men. He was
found not guilty, but so severely censured
that he resigned his commission.

The Zulu victory at Ntombe focussed Wood's attention on the need to displace the abaQulusi and Prince Mbilini from the strongholds to which they retired after each foray. In particular, he was keen to storm the Hlobane mountain, the largest and most secure of these strongholds. Since the abaQulusi regularly drove their herds on to the summit of the mountain, any such attack also had all the attractions of a particularly rich cattle raid. The mountain itself was a formidable obstacle, however, a flat-topped plateau 3 miles (5km) long, protected by a line of cliffs around the summit. There were only a few paths up through the cliffs – these the Zulu barricaded – and in any case British scouts had been unable to form a detailed impression of the terrain. In the event, however, the wider war impelled Wood to launch an attack for which he was not adequately prepared.

By the middle of March, a stream of British reinforcements was arriving at Durban, and Lord Chelmsford began to plan to recover the initiative from the Zulu. The easy confidence of the Isandlwana campaign had given way to a very real fear of Zulu capabilities, however, and Chelmsford was not prepared to take any further risks. His first military objective was to rescue Pearson's column from its investment at Eshowe, and towards the end of the month he had accumulated sufficient troops at the Lower Thukela to consider an advance. This build-up was quite obvious to Zulu scouts watching from distant hill-tops across the border, and Chelmsford hoped to make a number of diversionary attacks to confuse the Zulu regarding his true intentions. As a result, he ordered his garrison commanders along the length of the border to cross the river and inflict what damage they could on the Zulu.

These orders proved to be controversial. Apart from Wood's column in the north of the country, most of the garrisons guarding the remote border crossings were composed largely of colonial troops – white volunteers, and a black auxiliary unit known as the Border Levies. The Lieutenant-Governor of Natal, Bulwer, had always been reluctant to

allow Natal troops to serve in Zululand under British regulars, and he was particularly opposed to the idea of border raids, which would inevitably damage civilian, rather than military, targets, and provoke the Zulu into reprisals. Chelmsford got the better of this political tussle, but in the event most of the localised raids were small in scale – and produced exactly the result Bulwer feared. At Middle Drift, the local commander, Major Twentyman, was delayed by the state of the river, and could not cross into Zululand until 2 April. His men burned a few Zulu homesteads and retired with a herd of captured cattle. Insignificant as it was in itself, this incident was sufficient to begin a cycle of raid and counter-raid which continued almost to the end of the war.

It was this initiative on Chelmsford's part which also persuaded Wood to make his attack on the Hlobane complex.

The turning point

Throughout the middle of March, the evident British build-up on the borders had led King Cetshwayo to reassemble his army for a fresh campaign. The regiments had largely recovered from the shock of their losses at Isandlwana, and were confident that they could repeat their success if they could once again catch the British in the open. Although it seemed likely that the main British objective would be the relief of Eshowe, the Zulu high command felt that they had sufficient troops in the coastal sector, besieging the mission, to cope with a British advance on that front. They were, however, bombarded with messages from Prince Mbilini, the abaQulusi and the *amakhosi* of the northern chiefdoms begging for support to stop Wood and his rapacious raiding.

As a result, it was decided that the main army should this time be sent to the north. It consisted of the same regiments who had triumphed at Isandlwana, once more under the command of Ntshingwayo kaMahole. The king gave his commanders specific

A group of senior Zulu *izinduna* and their attendants, photographed after the war. Mahubulwana kaDumisela, the tall man in the centre, is one of the commanders of the abaQulusi section who fought at Hlobane; standing next to him is Mafunzi, one of King Cetshwayo's royal messengers. (Pietermaritzburg Archives Depot).

instructions on how they should approach the campaign. In particular, they should avoid the mistakes of Rorke's Drift, and rather than fight the British on ground of their own choosing – do not put your faces into the lair of the wild beasts, the king is said to have warned them, for you are sure to get clawed – they should try to lure them out by attacking the transport oxen when they were grazing. For the second time in the war, the army was ritually prepared, and it set off on 24 March for Wood's base at Khambula.

Ironically, news of the Zulu movements reached Wood as he was making his final preparations for the assault on Hlobane. He did not, however, regard the reports as unduly important, and in any case overestimated the time it would take for the Zulu army to reach him. He therefore decided to go ahead with the attack, confident that it would be long over before the Zulu army posed him any real threat.

Hlobane lay about 15 miles (24km) east of Wood's position at Khambula. Because of the distance involved, and the rugged nature of the terrain, Wood decided not to employ his British infantry, but to mount the assault with irregular cavalry and auxiliaries instead. One party, under Colonel Russell, was to ascend a hill known as Ntendeka, which abutted the western end of Hlobane, and then go on to the main mountain by what appeared from a distance to be a steep grassy slope, some 200 feet high, which connected them. The other party, under Colonel Buller, was to swing round to assault the far eastern end of the mountain, to secure the summit, and to drive the cattle corralled there to meet Russell at the other end. Both parties numbered over 600 men, including auxiliaries, and they set off after dark on the night of the 27th, so as to be in position to launch their attacks at dawn. Wood himself decided to follow Buller's party with his staff to observe how the attack developed.

Buller's party launched their assault just before daybreak the following morning, riding up a steep cattle track which wound up through the cliffs. A sudden thunderstorm broke overhead as they approached the cliffs,

and against this dramatic backdrop they came under fire from a few Zulu scouts posted on the summit above them. But Buller's men easily forced the passage, and as the sun rose they secured the eastern end of the mountain and began to drive off the small parties of Zulu guarding cattle on the summit. At the western end, Russell's party successfully climbed Ntendeka, but found that instead of a grassy slope, the pass connecting their position to the top of Hlobane was a steep staircase of rock. Russell decided it was impractical to lead horses up the pass, but he sent some of his auxiliaries up, and they too began to round up cattle.

Yet the abaQulusi had clearly been prepared for such a move. A large number of warriors had been living in temporary huts on the rugged northern foot of the mountain, and once they heard the sound of firing, they began to both work up towards the summit, and sweep round the foot of the

Lt. Col. Redvers Buller, Wood's resourceful cavalry commander. The irregular troops under Buller's command became accomplished raiders, but suffered heavily during the disastrous retreat from Hlobane on 28 March. (Ron Sheeley collection)

War in Northern Zululand

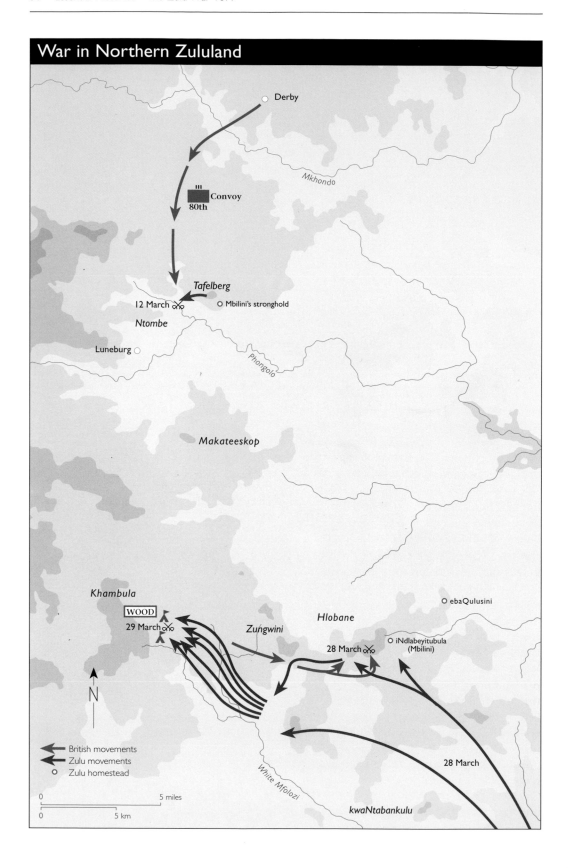

British movements
Zulu movements
Zulu homestead

0   5 miles
0   5 km

cliffs. Buller's rearguard soon found themselves engaged in a sporadic firefight with Zulu moving through the boulders below the cliffs, and soon the pass by which Buller had ascended was cut off. The first person to feel the effect of this was Wood himself. Following in Buller's path, he encountered a party or irregulars from Buller's command who had become separated during the dark ascent, and were now under heavy fire from Zulus concealed among boulders at the foot of the cliffs. Wood went forward to encourage the men on, and his staff promptly came under fire. His interpreter, a civilian named Lloyd, was killed, and Wood's own horse was shot. Wood's staff officer, Captain Campbell, led a rush towards the boulders, and was shot through the head, though the men following behind drove the Zulus further back into the crevices. Yet even as Wood took the bodies of his casualties a few hundred yards further down the slope to rebury them, the Zulu reoccupied their position.

Wood was unnerved by the loss of two members of his staff, and decided to return to Khambula. As he rode across the foot of

An aerial photograph of the Hlobane complex. Hlobane was one of a chain of mountains used as a refuge by the abaQulusi, and was unsuccessfully assaulted by the British on 28 March. This view shows the pass at the western end which connected Hlobane proper to the lower plateau, Ntendeka; Russell's party failed to ascend by this route at the beginning of the battle, while Buller's men were driven down it during the rout. (Private collection)

the mountain, an auxiliary with him urgently pointed to a range of hills to the south. A large column of Zulu was moving across country advancing rapidly towards Hlobane. It was the right wing of the main Zulu army, coming from oNdini; its appearance was largely coincidental, but the commanders had seen the fighting on the distant mountain-top, and had immediately rushed to join the battle.

The sight of the approaching army was soon apparent to all the scattered British groups on the mountain, who immediately recognised their danger. The summit of Hlobane was a natural trap; once on the top, the British had few ways off, and the abaQulusi had already reduced the options. As the Zulu column approached, it split in two, heading towards either end of the mountain.

In the confusion, one British party under a Colonel Weatherley attempted to retreat down the path Buller had come up; harried by the abaQulusi, they rode straight into the right horn of the Zulu army coming in the opposite direction. They tried to escape around the eastern end of Hlobane, only to find their way barred by a line of cliffs 200 feet high. Some were caught and killed by the Zulu above the cliffs; others simply rode over to their deaths, while a few managed to find a way down through the scree between the sheer cliff faces, and escaped.

Wood had warned Russell of the danger, ordering him to retire off the top of Ntendeka. Russell misinterpreted the order, and rode several miles further west, towards Khambula, leaving Buller's men unsupported on the summit of Hlobane itself. Driven in by abaQulusi, who were now streaming up on to the plateau in large numbers, Buller's command had no choice but to try to get down by the pass which Russell had earlier thought impractical. Here the men had to dismount and lead the horses from boulder to boulder, all the time under heavy attack from warriors who fired at them and threw spears from the boulders on either side, or rolled down rocks from the top. Despite Buller's gallant efforts, his command disintegrated, the survivors fleeing across country towards Khambula. The abaQulusi followed them for several miles, killing stragglers, until darkness brought an end to the pursuit.

For Wood, the foray had been a disaster. Over 90 of his irregulars had been killed, including Piet Uys, a farmer in the disputed territory, the only Boer of note to support the British invasion. No roll was completed of the auxiliaries' casualties, but they were at least equal to the white losses.

That night, the Zulu army regrouped and bivouacked to the west of Hlobane. It was all too obvious what their objective would be the following day.

The debacle at Hlobane did at least give Wood warning of the Zulu approach. At dawn the following morning, he stood the camp at Khambula to, and prepared to make a defence. He had chosen his position well for it lay along the crest of a narrow ridge, commanding an open slope to the north with an uninterrupted view of miles of country. To the south, the ground was much steeper, dropping away into the marshy streams which formed the headwaters of the White Mfolozi river. Wood had built a narrow earthwork on a high point on the ridge, and below it the camp was protected by two wagon *laagers*. Any attack would have to be made uphill, and except to the south, most of it would be completely exposed to British fire.

The importance of the coming battle was equally obvious for both sides. Early in the morning, Wood's scouts saw the Zulu approaching from their bivouac, then halt, and form into a circle for the last pre-battle rituals. Here they were addressed by *inkhosi* Mnyamana Buthelezi, the king's most senior councillor, who had accompanied the army in recognition of the vital nature of the campaign. Mnyamana was a powerful orator, who stressed the terrible repercussions which might flow from defeat. The Zulu had triumphed at Isandlwana, and if they won again at Khambula, they might dishearten the British, and cause them to abandon the invasion; yet if they lost, they would throw away all the advantages they had earlier gained. To the British inside the *laager*, watching as the Zulu *amabutho* deployed to take up a battle formation, the opposite was equally apparent.

Yet in their eagerness to get to grips with the enemy, the *amabutho* gave the battle to the British. Whatever King Cetshwayo's intentions, the army, keen to resolve the issue, had no patience for subtle strategies to lure the British away from their defences. The two horns pressed out on either side, and swung round to surround the British camp. To the south, the left horn entered the valley below the camp and disappeared from sight, its approach hidden by the falling ground. To Wood's surprise, it took a long time to emerge – slowed by the marshy ground, it literally bogged down. In the meantime, however, the right horn was plainly visible as it took up a position a couple of miles away to the north.

Wood realised that the Zulu approach was already becoming uncoordinated, and that if he could provoke the right horn into launching a premature attack, he might be able to concentrate his fire on each assault in turn, rather than being attacked on all sides at once. The irregular horsemen – most of them survivors of Hlobane – were sent out to provoke the right horn to attack. They rode down the open slope, dismounted just 50 yards from the Zulu line, and opened fire. The Zulu promptly rushed forward – some of the colonials in the camp heard them calling out 'We are the boys from Isandlwana!' – scattering the horsemen before them, chasing them back towards the nearest *laager*. Once the horsemen were clear of the line of fire, the British opened a devastating fusillade. With no cover or concealment, the Zulu were shot down in droves. Some elements reached the wall of wagons, only to be driven back; they hung on for a while, unable to cross the last few yards to the British lines, then reluctantly they retreated, rallying behind a fold in the ground which offered them some protection from the storm.

The noise of this first attack brought the left horn hurrying up from the valley. They remained out of sight of the British positions until they emerged at the head of the slope just two or three hundred yards from the *laagers*. Although exposed to rifle fire from those positions, and from field guns which Wood now turned to meet them, they succeeded in reaching the nearest British position and secured the crest-line. Here, a few hundred yards to their left, the Zulu occupied a patch of long grass and mealies which had sprouted on the camp dung heap. Zulu armed with British rifles taken at Isandlwana were able to fire down into Wood's position, and in particular to enfilade part of the smaller of the two *laagers*, which lay to the south of the central redoubt. When a company holding that line was forced to withdraw, the Zulu immediately followed them up, and succeeded in driving the British right out of the *laager*.

This was the crucial point in the battle. The dung heap and captured *laager* between them secured the flanks of the Zulu approaching up the valley slope between them, and there was a very real chance that they might assemble in sufficient numbers to support a successful assault on the main *laager* nearby. Wood recognised the danger, and ordered two companies of the 90th Regiment, under the command of Major Robert Hackett, to make a sortie from the main *laager* to the head of the slope. The infantry marched out in impressive style, catching the Zulu by surprise, and forcing the nearest elements to retire down the slope. Once in position, Hackett's men deployed in line and opened a heavy fire on the left horn sheltering below them. Hackett's men were in turn caught by a galling fire from the dung heap and captured *laager* on either side, and indeed Hackett himself was severely wounded. Wood recalled them, but the move had been determined enough to discourage the left horn from launching its attack. The British then directed volley after volley from the main *laager* into the soft dung heap, flattening it and suppressing the Zulu fire.

In the meantime, the Zulu centre had approached Khambula from the east, streaming across the open ridge, only to be met with the same heavy fire that had broken the other attacks. In some places Zulu dead fell against the slopes of the redoubt itself, but the centre was no more successful than either horn before them. For three more hours, the Zulu continued to attack the camp, even the right horn rallying for one more assault. Yet the attacks were mounted piecemeal, and each repulse added to British confidence and disheartened the Zulu. By late afternoon, the Zulu began to prepare to withdraw. Wood, seeing them retire in good order, took the opportunity to deliver one final blow – the mounted irregulars were sent out to drive the Zulu from the field. Most of the Zulu were by this time exhausted, and some were so tired they could not lift their shields to defend themselves. The irregulars cut them down

with a ruthlessness born of the horrors of Hlobane, and as the Zulu army drifted away, it began to break up. The irregulars pursued them across 7 miles (11km) of countryside before night afforded the Zulu some relief.

The importance of the British victory was immediately obvious to everyone at Khambula. Some 785 Zulu bodies were collected from around the camp, and buried in mass graves nearby; hundreds more lay on the line of retreat, their whereabouts marked for days by circling vultures and crows. In all, the Zulu death toll at Khambula probably exceeded that of Isandlwana, while the

wounded faced long, agonising journeys through the sparsely populated northern districts towards home. Hundreds died along the way. *Inkhosi* Mnyamana tried to urge the army to return to oNdini, to report to the king, as was traditional, but most of the warriors were too dispirited, and simply made their way to their own homes. Temporarily, at least, the battle had effectively destroyed the Zulu army.

The British, by contrast, had suffered just three officers and 25 men dead, and five officers and 50 men wounded. Wood's timely victory had rescued his own reputation from

the implications of his poor judgement at Hlobane – and with it restored British prestige in Zululand.

The war on the coast

For the Zulu, there was worse to come. On the same day that Wood fought at Khambula, Chelmsford had finally begun his advance to relieve Eshowe. He had collected over 5,000 men at the Lower Thukela including three infantry battalions who had recently arrived as reinforcements from

Britain. He had decided to accompany the column in person, and was determined to make none of the mistakes of the Isandlwana campaign. The continued wet weather, worse in the coastal sector than up-country, continued to make progress slow, but in any case Chelmsford insisted that each halt be properly protected. Each night, the columns were drawn into a *laager* – the British preferred a square formation, rather than the traditional Boer circle – which was surrounded by a shelter trench and rampart. While the transport animals and auxiliaries slept inside the *laager*, the troops slept between the wagons and the trench, ready to man the rampart in case of attack. Some of the battalions fresh out from the UK had been made up to strength with new recruits, and the stories which had circulated since Isandlwana had created a climate of unease which would prevail throughout the rest of the campaign, so that the advance was made somewhat apprehensively.

Once it became clear that the anticipated British advance had begun, the Zulu concentrated in the hills around Eshowe began to move out to oppose Chelmsford's column. They took up a position along the valley of the Nyezane river – the same spot where Pearson had been attacked two months before – which effectively blocked Chelmsford's road.

On 1 April the relief column reached a low grassy rise near the ruins of the kwaGingindlovu homestead, which Pearson had earlier destroyed on his way past. Their objective was not far ahead; below them, the track dropped gently down towards the Nyezane, rising up steeply on the far side to the green hills of Eshowe beyond. As usual, the column formed an entrenched *laager*. At dawn the next morning, as a dense mist began to lift in the valley below, British

Inkhosi Somopho kaZikhala, the senior *induna* at the emaNgweni royal homestead north of Eshowe, and the man who commanded the unsuccessful Zulu attack on the British at Gingindlovu. (MuseuMAfrica)

outposts saw a Zulu force emerging from it and steadily advancing to attack.

The Zulu numbered about 11,000 men, and were commanded by Somopho kaZikhala, an *induna* of one of the most important royal homesteads in the coastal districts. Under him were several important officers who had fought in the Isandlwana campaign, including Mavumengwana kaNdlela, who had been co-commander in that battle, and Prince Dabulamanzi, the unsuccessful commander at Rorke's Drift.

The Zulu deployed in their usual encircling movement, making a determined attack against the front right corner of Chelmsford's square. This attack almost succeeded, since it unnerved many of the young recruits in the British line, and reached to within 50 yards before collapsing. The Zulu then spread out in the long grass, circling to the British left, searching for a way in. In the meantime, the Zulu right had come into action, sweeping round to attack the rear of the position. This attack, too, was repulsed, the momentum carrying the warriors round to the far side of the square. Here they rallied in hollows protected from the British fire, but when they again advanced and were exposed to British musketry, they were shot down in scores. The British, indeed, commanded a zone of fire around the *laager* which the Zulu found it impossible to penetrate. After perhaps an hour, the Zulu began to withdraw, and Chelmsford ordered his mounted detachments to pursue them. At first, the Zulu attempted to stand, but when the NNC were sent to support the cavalry, the Zulus broke and fled.

As at Khambula, the British pursuit was severe, the troops made vengeful by their relief and by having inflicted a defeat on such a terrifying enemy. Many wounded and exhausted Zulu were cut down as they tried to cross the Nyezane river. Nearly 500 Zulu bodies were found around the *laager* site, and several

hundred more lay concealed in the long grass beyond. Some sources put the tally of Zulu dead as high as 1,000 men; the British, by contrast, lost just two officers and 12 men killed, and four officers and 43 men wounded.

The following day Lord Chelmsford marched to relieve the garrison at Eshowe. Pearson's men had endured nearly three months of hardship, and over 30 of the garrison had died of disease. To the disappointment of the Eshowe garrison, however, Lord Chelmsford had already decided not to hold the post. As he had discovered, it was too far advanced to protect and supply adequately, and he intended to retire with the entire force to a point much closer to the Thukela, while he reorganised his invasion plan. After one last gesture of defiance – the destruction of Prince Dabulamanzi's personal homestead, which lay nearby – the British dismantled their fort at Eshowe, abandoned the mission buildings to the Zulu, and withdrew.

The battle of Gingindlovu, 2 April; a sketch by Capt. C.P. Cramer, 60th Regiment. As the mist clears in the Nyezane valley, the Zulu army deploys to attack Lord Chelmsford's square. (Killie Campbell Library)

Fighting for the empire

For many ordinary soldiers in the British ranks, the Anglo-Zulu War meant long periods of discomfort, long marches in baking heat or pouring rain, poor food and bad water, a regimented routine lived briefly in an alien and often frightening environment, and perhaps occasionally the sudden terror and adrenalin rush of combat. Although literacy standards were rising in the 1870s, and many letters from individual soldiers have survived, their accounts of the war are seldom as complete or easy to document as those of their officers. The officer class was not only well-educated in an age when both letter-writing and diaries were fashionable, but their rank often gave them a greater variety of duties and wider understanding of the war as a whole.

Captain William Cochrane

William Francis Dundonald Cochrane's experiences of the campaign were among the most varied – and dramatic. He was born into the rural gentry in the county of Wiltshire, in the UK, in 1847. He joined the 32nd (Duke of Cornwall's) Light Infantry in 1866 as an Ensign – the lowest officer's rank. When Lord Chelmsford appealed in late 1878 for reinforcements for the coming Zulu campaign, there was a rush of enthusiastic young officers to volunteer for any special service posts which might be available. Promotion for officers in the peacetime Victorian Army was notoriously slow, and after 12 years' service Cochrane was still

languishing in the rank of lieutenant. A war offered not only the possibility of adventure, butalso of promotion and distinction, so he volunteered; having previously travelled in Natal, he was accepted, and sailed for Durban on the steamship *Edinburgh Castle*.

British mounted infantry pursuing fleeing Zulus during the closing stages of the battle of Gingindlovu on 2 April. This defeat, coming just days after the British victory at Khambula, dispersed the main Zulu concentrations at either end of the country, and marked a turning point in the war. (Private collection)

On board were a number of young officers in the same position as himself, several of whom were to play a prominent part in the early stages of the war. Among them was Lieutenant Henry Harford, 99th Regiment, who was attached to the staff of the 3rd NNC, and would leave a graphic description of the Isandlwana campaign. Lieutenant Horace Smith-Dorrien, 95th Regiment, would be destined to escape from Isandlwana, while Lieutenant Charles Williams, 58th Regiment, would be killed in the attack on Hlobane. According to Harford, Cochrane excelled at the sort of pastimes which were then popular among the British officer class:

Cochrane was simply the life and soul of the ship, always ready to sit down at the piano and sing a good song, or get up concerts, theatricals and other amusements. Scarcely a day went by without something going on under his direction.

On arriving in Natal, Cochrane was appointed transport officer to Colonel Anthony Durnford's No. 2 Column. Under

Captain William Cochrane, photographed at the turn of the century. Cochrane was a regular officer in the 32nd Regiment, who volunteered for special service in Zululand. Attached to Durnford's column, he survived Isandlwana – and went on to take part in the battles of Hlobane, Khambula and Ulundi. (Pietermaritzburg Archives Depot)

Chelmsford's original invasion plan, this column was given a defensive role on the central Thukela border, above Middle Drift. Durnford's column consisted almost entirely of African auxiliary troops, supported by an artillery rocket battery. Once Chelmsford himself had crossed the border into Zululand, however, Durnford's column was ordered up to Rorke's Drift to support the advance. On the morning of the 22nd, Durnford received Chelmsford's order to advance to Isandlwana. Cochrane accompanied Durnford when he entered the camp at about 10.30 am, and overheard the conversation in which Colonel Pulleine reported the Zulu presence to the left of the camp. According to Cochrane, Durnford replied that he would 'go out and prevent the one column from joining the [Zulu army], which was supposed to be at that time engaged with the troops under the General'.

Cochrane again accompanied Durnford, whose party rode about 5 miles (8km) from the camp when they suddenly encountered the Zulu left horn, approaching from the opposite direction. They retired fighting, and took up a position in a *donga* some distance in front of the camp. After defending this for a while, however, Cochrane recalled that

A general move was made towards the mountain, to take up a last position, but it was too late; the Zulus were too quick and fleet of foot, they caught up with the men on foot before they could reach the new position, completely overpowering them by numbers, and assegaing right and left …

As far as I am personally concerned, when I got back to camp with the mounted men who had been driven out of the 'donga', I found that the enemy rushed on the camp from the left, and were engaged hand-to-hand with the infantry, who were completely overpowered with overwhelming numbers. I saw that all was over. I made in the direction which I had seen taken by the mounted men, guns, Royal Artillery, and the natives on foot. I was cut off by the enemy, who had now reached the line of retreat; but with a good horse, hard riding, and good luck, I managed to reach the Buffalo River. The Zulus seemed perfectly fearless; they following alongside, having desperate hand-to-hand fighting with those retreating, mostly our natives on foot. Many of the

enemy were killed between the camp and the river. On several occasions they were quite close to me, but I was fortunate enough to escape, whilst others dropped at my side. They fired at us the whole way from the camp to the river, but having mounted the bank on the opposite side we were safe.

Years later, Cochrane would recall ruefully that he escaped Isandlwana by 'damn all but the ears of my horse'. He made his way to Helpmekaar, on the hills beyond Rorke's Drift. That night, and for several days thereafter, the garrison at Helpmekaar lived in expectation of a Zulu attack, and if that attack never came, life was still far from pleasant. Survivors from Isandlwana huddled together with the garrison behind makeshift barricades, often lying in the mud on wet nights. Those who had escaped the battle had lost everything but the uniforms they stood up in – greatcoats, tents, blankets and personal possessions. Many were so traumatised by their experiences that they cried out in their sleep, setting off a series of false alarms.

Gradually, however, the terror subsided, and once it became clear that the Zulu were not intending to mount an immediate attack, the British began to secure the border once more. With the death of Colonel Durnford and the destruction of his column, Cochrane's position as transport officer was superfluous. On 20 February he was given the local rank of captain and was appointed to the command of two of the troops of mounted auxiliaries from the centre column – the Edendale Christian contingent and Hlubi's Sotho detachment – which had remained in the field near Rorke's Drift. Lord Chelmsford had by now begun to reorganise his forces in the aftermath of Isandlwana, and Cochrane's command was attached to Colonel Wood's column in the north, riding into Khambula on 1 March.

Ironically, these survivors of Isandlwana now found themselves in the thick of the next wave of fighting. When Colonel Wood decided to attack Hlobane, Cochrane's men

African auxiliaries from one of the mounted units who fought for the British. The mounted 'Native Contingent' were considered to be the best of the auxiliary troops; they were generally known to the British as 'Basutos', although in fact only a few were of Sotho origin. Cochrane commanded men such as these during the closing stages of the war. (Private collection)

were attached to Russell's column, which was ordered to attack the western end of the mountain. Russell successfully ascended the Ntendeka plateau, but found it impossible to reach the main summit. His men waited at the foot of the pass until the sound of firing could be heard from Buller's party across the summit, and numbers of Zulu began to gather to snipe at Russell's command. Cochrane's men were ordered to dismount and drive them off. With the news that a much larger Zulu army was approaching, however, Russell decided to abandon the mountain altogether. For a while, he kept his mounted men lined up at the foot of Ntendeka; then, receiving a confusing order from Wood, he retired several miles away, towards Khambula. By this movement he left Buller's men – and some of his own auxiliaries, who had been herding cattle – unsupported.

The incident later caused much bitterness towards Russell, and it may have affected the behaviour of Cochrane's men the following day. When the Zulu army first deployed to attack Khambula, the mounted auxiliaries were among those who rode out to sting the right horn into action. Most rode back to take refuge in the main wagon *laager*, but according to one eye-witness:

The Basutos [the British habitually referred to all their black mounted troops as such], who had stuck like leeches to the cattle on Hlobane the day before and brought them off safely, left the laager and refused to stay. Throughout the fight they hovered round the flank of the Zulus firing continually.

In the aftermath of the victory at Khambula, Cochrane's men were extensively employed in patrolling. Once Lord Chelmsford began to plan the new invasion, this included long-range reconnaissances into Zulu territory in search of a viable road to oNdini. Skirmishes with Zulu scouts were common, and one irregular officer left a vivid account of such actions, which must have been very familiar to Cochrane:

We were reconnoitering some six miles over the Zulu border, and were suddenly fired on; the Basutos loosed off in all directions wildly, they were so excited. The scene was characteristic, the Zulus shouting challenges

to the Basutos to come up the hill, the
Basutos challenging the Zulus to come
down; both parties fired at random, and the
only damage done was a broken rifle-stock,
which a huge bullet from an elephant gun
had shivered. The Basutos used to level their
guns over their horses' heads with one hand
and fire wildly; they are nevertheless capital
Irregulars, the best scouts in the world,
hardy, active, and enduring, their only
faults are their excitability and their
random firing.

On 1 June, a patrol from the 2nd
Division was attacked in a deserted Zulu
homestead on the Tshotshozi river. The
survivors fled towards Wood's column, and
the following morning a large detachment
of mounted men were sent out to search for
the bodies. Ironically, Cochrane again
found himself present at a historic moment:
'About the same distance lower down in the
main donga,' wrote an observer, 'lay
another body perfectly nude, with Captain
Cochrane standing guard over it. I at once

recognised it as the corpse of the ex-Prince Imperial of France.'

For a further month, Chelmsford's columns continued to advance into the heart of Zululand. The irregular cavalry – and with them Cochrane's men – took part in the skirmishes which marked their progress. On 3 July, when Buller's men crossed the White Mfolozi to scout out positions for the coming battle of Ulundi, the Edendale and Sotho troops accompanied the reconnaissance. When the British were ambushed, these troops found themselves in the rearguard, and at one point were almost cut off. As they broke through the Zulu cordon, the Zulus called out 'tomorrow we will drive you across the river, and we will eat up all the red soldiers'. The following day, however, the auxiliaries had their revenge:

Cochrane's Basutos distinguished themselves at the battle of Ulundi by their dash. They were ordered by Colonel Buller to draw on the Zulus from the right side of the square. Instead of firing a few shots and falling back, they made a stand and poured volley after volley into the advancing masses of the enemy. When told to retreat they asked their officers what was now to become of them? They were under the impression that they had to remain outside the square, and wait patiently until they were all killed ...but when they drew near the glittering line of bayonets and saw the veteran 13th open a way for them to enter the square, they saw that they were not to be aimlessly sacrificed. When they had dismounted they asked the soldiers what they had to do. 'Eat your biscuits, Johnny, and lie down' ...

A few minutes after the Lancers swept out from the left corner of the rear, the Basutos dashed out at the right corner of the front ... they shouted out after the very same [Zulu] regiment that had chased them [earlier] the ironical words, 'Well, are you going to the [river] now?' ... During the

chase one of the Basutos shot a Zulu in the leg, and then interviewed the man with all the thirst for news which distinguishes a New York reporter ... Then he gently asked the Zulu if he had got nothing more to tell, and on being assured that there was no more information to be had, he quietly shot the man, mounted his horse, and joined again in the chase.

The battle of Ulundi marked the end of the Anglo-Zulu War for Cochrane. While the auxiliaries under his command were

disbanded, and returned to their ordinary lives in colonial Natal, Cochrane, the professional soldier, went on to serve in a number of Queen Victoria's many wars. He fought with colonial forces in South Africa again in the BaSotho 'Gun War' of 1880–81, and the following year served at the other end of the continent, when British troops quelled an anti-European revolt in Egypt. In 1893 he was given a brigade command in the reorganised Anglo-Egyptian army, and he took part in the early stages of the conquest of the Sudan in 1896.

Throughout his career, Cochrane took part in the wide range of combat which in many ways typified the experience of Victorian officers. Nothing, however, would ever compare to the ordeal of his escape from Isandlwana.

He died in London in 1928 with the rank of brigadier-general.

'Shepstone's Horse' – commanded by Cochrane – sketched in action at the beginning of the battle of Ulundi on 4 July. The unit played a prominent part in the battle, provoking the Zulu to attack the British square, and later taking part in the pursuit. (National Army Museum)

Reaction to the war

On 12 March 1879, the Right Reverend John Colenso, Bishop of Natal, delivered a sermon in the colonial capital of Pietermaritzburg to honour the dead of Isandlwana. Colenso was an ardent humanitarian, whose support for the African standpoint had often made him unpopular among the settler community, and his speech on this occasion was no exception. So far from being the necessary pre-emptive strike portrayed by Frere, Colenso saw the war as a tragedy, an unnecessary and unjust act of aggression by the British Empire against a people who had struggled to remain on good terms with them. Colenso was certainly not alone in his stance. Many in colonial society had misgivings about the war, and influential groups in the UK – such as the Aborigines Protection Society – were also deeply uncomfortable about British policies. The actions of both Frere and Lord Chelmsford had come under some scrutiny in the British Parliament.

Yet these were undoubtedly minority views. In Natal, many settlers had been personally affected by the colonial losses at Isandlwana, and a desire for revenge was widespread. Isandlwana, too, had aroused the deep-seated fear and hostility of many of Natal's African groups towards the Zulu Royal House, while in Britain the Zulu people – unknown to the public a few months before – were demonised in the illustrated press. Isandlwana, far from being a contest sought equally by both armies in the field, was presented as a ruthless and treacherous massacre. The Zulu were portrayed as a wild and exotic people who, like Africa itself, needed to be tamed and made safe in the name of civilised progress. With the majority of the literate public squarely behind the war, the government was content to support British troops in the field, at least until British prestige was restored.

Yet, for all the determination to avenge the British defeat, the war remained something of an embarrassment to the government. Disraeli's Conservative administration had been characterised by an expansionist approach to the Empire, and by 1879 the implications of this were creating an undercurrent of political opposition. In 1875, taking advantage of the financial difficulties of the Khedive of Egypt, the British government had purchased a controlling interest in the Suez Canal. Although this afforded some strategic security – the Canal greatly reduced travelling times to British India – it had led to increased involvement in Egyptian affairs which, within a few years, would require armed intervention. And in India, over which Queen Victoria had recently taken the title Empress, the British had adopted an aggressive policy with regard to Russian intervention in Afghanistan on the north-western border. When the Amir of Afghanistan had been persuaded to allow a Russian envoy into the Afghan capital at Kabul, the British had demanded a similar privilege. The Amir had refused, so British and Indian troops had invaded Afghanistan in November 1878. Although the British advance was rapid and successful, fighting continued throughout the early part of 1879, just as the most dangerous phase of the war was developing in Zululand. The British Army therefore found itself fighting two very different wars at the same time. Nor was the 2nd Afghan War a minor affair, it being waged under the constant threat that it might provoke a direct confrontation with Russian forces in central Asia, a fear that had dominated British strategy on India's western borders for half a century. The war came to a temporary halt when the Amir accepted the presence of a British Resident, but the massacre of the latter by a Kabul mob in September provoked a fresh wave of fighting. In the course of that fighting, a British column was largely wiped out at the battle of Maiwand in July 1880 – an action which had much in common with Isandlwana, though it was not quite so costly. The 2nd Afghan War did not end until August 1880 – and against such a background, many British officials had regarded Frere's decision to provoke a quarrel with the Zulu as an irritating distraction.

The two wars also led to the emergence of two distinct groupings within the British Army, two rival schools of influence and preferment, based upon the informal associations of officers who served in the different wars – the 'India school' and the 'Africa school'. When the Anglo-Boer War broke out in 1899, requiring a far greater commitment of troops than any before in the Victorian period, and the involvement of officers from both schools, the divisions between them often led to confusion in the field.

Towards the end of 1879, Disraeli's political rival, the Liberal leader William Gladstone, began to campaign against the Conservatives, attacking their record in the Empire in particular. Gladstone argued that the war in Afghanistan had been unnecessary, and that in Zululand unjust. 'What was the crime of the Zulus?' Gladstone asked with powerful rhetoric, marshalling growing misgivings among the literate voting classes in Britain, to the extent that in April 1880 the Disraeli administration fell – another victim, in its way, of Isandlwana.

For the most part, however, the war aroused little interest in the wider world. Rival European powers regarded it as another British foreign adventure at a time when most world powers entertained ambitions to increase their Imperial possessions. The death of the French Prince Imperial on 1 June created a minor stir in Anglo-French relations; the French republican government, who had derided the prince during his lifetime, warmed to him on his death, using the incident as another means to embarrass their traditional rivals, the British. Yet the

political implications of the prince's death remain imponderable; he might, indeed, have been destined to lead his country to a golden future as the Emperor Napoleon IV, with whatever repercussions that might have had on the eve of a new century in which Germany came to dominate European affairs. But in fact Bonapartism was already a political anachronism in France by 1879, and the wave of sentiment which greeted the prince's death had more to do with nostalgia than with a realistic hope of restoration. Probably, had he lived, the young prince would have been doomed to the empty life of the ruler in exile, moving from one glittering watering hole to another, awaiting a call to return which would never come.

It was in South Africa that the effects of the war were most felt. Ironically, in the light of Frere's hopes that a successful Zulu campaign would cement British authority in the region, the disaster at Isandlwana had the opposite effect. As news of the British defeat spread, colonial officials became concerned that it would provoke a wave of sympathetic risings against white rule among other African groups. In fact, this did not happen, largely because those groups who had already committed themselves to the British cause felt compromised in Zulu eyes. The Natal chiefdoms remained behind the war, fearing a Zulu counter-attack. The Swazi kingdom, which had refused to openly ally themselves with the British, nestled even further into its perch on the political fence – a position it would only abandon at the very end of the war, once the British recovery was assured. Groups such as the Pedi, on the north-eastern borders of the Transvaal, who had been in dispute with white authority before the war began, remained so; yet they were too geographically distant, had too few resources, and simply had too little in common to provide a united front with the Zulu.

For the Boers the situation was more complex. Instead of demonstrating the security benefits of British rule, Isandlwana merely showed that the most powerful army in the world was by no means invulnerable – while at the same time increasing the risk of raids on the exposed frontier communities. The defeat encouraged republican sentiment to the extent that Colonel Rowlands was ordered from his reserve column on the Swazi–Zulu border and sent to Pretoria to watch for signs of dissent. The Boers were reluctant to make any overt attempt at rebellion while there were so many British troops in South Africa, however, and it was only in late 1880, when most of the redcoats had dispersed, that they broke into armed uprising.

By that time, the Confederation policy was long dead. Isandlwana had led to a searching analysis of Frere's actions in the British Parliament, and Gladstone had singled him out for particular criticism. Even while the fighting progressed, support for the scheme within white South Africa ebbed away, and Frere found himself largely isolated by Wolseley's appointment as the senior military and political officer at the Cape. With the fall of the Disraeli administration, Frere's days were numbered, and in August 1880 he was recalled. His dismissal marked the official end of the Confederation policy, and the beginning of a period of British retrenchment in South Africa. The Liberals refused to countenance the annexation of Zululand, and in the wake of the Boer revolt they would abandon the Transvaal.

Zulu attitudes towards the war

When Sir Bartle Frere drafted his ultimatum which instigated the British invasion, he was careful to draw a distinction between the administration of King Cetshwayo and the Zulu people themselves. The British, he said, were invading Zululand to punish the king; any Zulu civilians who chose to surrender would be welcomed by British troops. Partly, this was a necessary propaganda fiction, a reinforcement of Frere's stance that Cetshwayo was a despot who did not enjoy widespread support within the country. Partly, there was a very real hope that by being offered easy terms for surrender, ordinary Zulus could be persuaded to abandon their loyalty to the king, and that resistance would then collapse. Throughout the war, although the British were ruthless in the treatment of warriors in the heat of battle, they were careful not to mistreat Zulu civilians. Nevertheless, the fact that the war was fought entirely on Zulu soil meant that in those areas affected by the fighting the impact on civilian life was considerable. Ordinary Zulu homesteads suffered the depredations of foragers on both sides, and during the later stages of the war – civilian support having conspicuously failed to collapse – Lord Chelmsford took a deliberate decision to destroy both huts and food stores in the hope that hunger would undermine the Zulu resolve.

A remarkable insight into the war of an ordinary Zulu family is offered by the account of a young boy named Muziwento. Muziwento's story was written down by a white missionary and published in 1883, in both Zulu and English translation, under the title *A Zulu Boy's Recollections of the Zulu War*.

Muziwento's family lived close to the Isandlwana hill, and his people fell under the administration of *inkhosi* Sihayo kaXongo. Both Muziwento's father and his elder brothers had been enrolled in the king's *amabutho*, but Muziwento was not yet old enough, and in January 1879 was still herding his father's cattle at home. The arrival of the British centre column at Rorke's Drift, opposite Sihayo's territory, caused some concern among the Zulu at large. Some were openly contemptuous of the British forces, while others argued that the non-combatants should be evacuated to strongholds as a precaution. When the centre column crossed into Zululand on 11 January, and attacked Sihayo's followers the following day, many of the civilians living in the Isandlwana district abandoned their homes, driving their herds first towards the Malakatha mountain, and then further off towards Siphezi. Although some were disconcerted by the sacking of Sihayo's homestead, and were keen to surrender, Miziwento's father was adamant; 'whosoever desires to do homage, it is good that he be off, and go and do homage [to the whites]', Muziwento recalled him saying. Some did, but about this time both Muziwento's father and his brothers left their family, and went to oNdini to join their regiments.

Siphezi mountain, where Muziwento was then staying, played a crucial role in the Isandlwana campaign. The main Zulu army passed by and camped on the slopes of the mountain on the night of 20/21 January, before moving closer to Isandlwana. The army had set out from oNdini with limited provisions, but these were becoming exhausted as it reached the front, and the men were dependent on foraging for survival. Muziwento had decidedly mixed feelings about this aspect of the war, feeling sympathetic towards the warriors and their cause, but troubled by the loss of family livestock. He recalled a small band of warriors going past early one morning: 'it

Zulu civilians photographed at the time of the war – a married man (standing left) and his family. Most men of fighting age took part in the war, and as the war pressed deeper and deeper into Zulu territory their dependents fled the proximity of British columns to hide in the hills. (Private collection)

being very cold indeed. One of them was chilled with the cold; he had no longer any power to get along quickly...He warmed himself at the fire. The others derided him.' He remembered, too, a party of foragers looming out of the mist, and seizing a number of sheep 'belonging to our father and other people'. They stabbed a number of these and took the carcasses off to feed the army, but when they tried to take a particularly fine kid, Muziwento's uncle objected, and a passing *induna* scolded the warriors, who moved on.

Muziwento was still at Siphezi when the battle of Isandlwana was fought, 15 miles (24km) away. Later, he heard tales of the battle from both his father and brothers, of the spontaneous nature of the Zulu attack, of the confused fighting, and the desperate

British resistance. Muziwento's father fought 'carrying a black and white shield. They shot at him; they hit it. He cast it away from him; he fought on with assegais and rifle only.' One of Muziwento's brothers, Mtweni, killed a white man whom the Zulu later believed to be George Shepstone, Durnford's staff officer, in hand-to-hand fighting among the rocks at the foot of Isandlwana hill.

Muziwento also heard a graphic account of the action at Rorke's Drift, told to him by one of the warriors of the uThulwana *ibutho*, Munyu, who was present. 'They stabbed the sacks,' he said of the attackers, 'they dug with their assegais. They were struck; they died. They set fire to the house. It was no longer fighting; they were now exchanging salutations only.' To most Zulu civilians, the fight at Rorke's Drift had seemed futile, and, unlike their British counterparts, they were unimpressed with the bravery of their own men who had fought there. 'The

A Zulu family photographed in a studio in 1879. The heavy casualties suffered by Zulu armies in the field affected all levels of Zulu society. (Private collection)

[uThulwana] regiment was finished up at Jim's – shocking cowards they were, too. Our people laughed at them,' said Muziwento. Nevertheless, he noted that most Zulu were wary of British fortifications after the battle. 'The Zulus had no desire to go to Maritzburg,' he said, 'they said "There are strongholds there".'

Muziwento's father had returned to his homestead after the battle, taking with him some sheep he had captured in the camp. Once the British had retired to the border, Muziwento and his family also returned home. The young boys could not resist visiting the battlefield, despite the scolding of adults who were afraid of British reprisals. Muziwento was lured not only by the spectacle of the dead, but by the many treasures of European manufacture still lying on the field. His apocalyptic account of the stricken field ranks among the most vivid descriptions to come out of the war:

We went to see the dead people at Isandlwana. We saw a single warrior dead, staring in our direction, with his war shield in his hand. We ran away. We came back again. We saw countless things dead. Dead was the horse, dead too the mule, dead was the dog, dead was the monkey, dead were the wagons, dead were the tents, dead were the boxes, dead was everything, even to the very metals.

Scared off by the warnings of adults and the distant sight of British patrols, Muziwento and his friends were still drawn back to the battlefield time and again, exploring the carnage and taking their choice of the debris where they dared.

When fighting resumed again in March, Muziwento's father again took part. *Inkhosi* Sihayo's people had links with Prince Mbilini, for one of Sihayo's sons fought with him in the guerrilla actions around Luneburg. From these sources, Muziwento heard of the Zulu success at Hlobane – 'they got a few white men, but the rest ran away' – and the defeat at Khambula. 'A good number of white men died, but the Zulus were

beaten,' recalled Muziwento sadly, 'great numbers of them perished.'

With the increased British dominance around Khambula – which was within striking distance of Sihayo's northern borders – the Zulu non-combatants were again moved away. They moved first to the district around eZungeni – where Sihayo's followers skirmished with British cavalry on 5 June – and then eastwards on to the Mthonjaneni heights. From here, as the British continued their inexorable advance, they moved down into the valley of the White Mfolozi, towards the cluster of royal homesteads at oNdini, where the gathering army afforded the greatest hope of security.

When the last great battle of the war took place there on 4 July, Muziwento's older kin were once more heavily involved:

Our father – they shot at him. He entered into a hole. He stayed there a little time. He arose and fled. Our brother too was present. He was an officer. He carried a breech-loading rifle that he had taken at Isandlwana from his [enemies]. The Zulu army fled. He got tired of running away. He was a man who understood well how to shoot. He shouted, 'back again!' He turned and fired. He struck a horse; it fell among the stones and the white man with it. All the white men turned upon him. They fired at him. They killed him.

The Zulu collapse at oNdini left the civilian population stunned. The extent of the defeat seemed incomprehensible, and Muziwento recalled a popular story that the British had been able to triumph so spectacularly only because they had thrown up a temporary barricade of iron sheeting around their positions. In the distance, Muziwento saw the clouds of smoke from the royal homesteads, which the British had destroyed: 'O! We flung away the clothes which we had taken at Isandlwana. We thought, perhaps we shall be put in prison by the white men on account of the clothes which we were wearing.' The dispirited civilians moved north, away from the

British. Out of their own districts, however, they found themselves the subject of anger and resentment from other Zulus who blamed *inkhosi* Sihayo for having provoked the British invasion.

Some time later, while Muziwento's family were still living in caves, a British patrol approached them, trying to induce them to surrender. The soldiers held up a letter at a distance as proof of their mission, but the Zulu remained wary, and one of Muziwento's brothers, who had fought with the uKhandempemvu regiment, approached them carrying a conspicuous stabbing spear. The troops drew off, and when their appeals to talk to a senior man went unanswered, they abandoned the attempt and rode away. Yet by this time large numbers of *izinduna* and warriors had begun to surrender at the British camp at oNdini, and Muziwento's family eventually submitted, receiving papers which allowed them to pass through British patrols on their way home.

Muziwento's father returned to his homestead at Isandlwana, taking what remained of his cattle with him, and later the family heard that Cetshwayo had been captured. There was a sense of relief in the country at large; although most Zulu remained loyal to the king, 'the people were sick of war'. Another son of Sihayo – Mehlokazulu, who had led the raid to recover his father's wives, which had been cited in the British ultimatum – was arrested by the troops and taken to Pietermaritzburg for trial, but later released. The family tried to resume their former way of life, but the war had cost them dearly. One brother had been killed in action, and several of those who fought were exhausted by the experience. One, recalled Muziwento, 'was ill for a long time; after a while he died'.

Sadly, for Muziwento and thousands like him, the greatest trial was yet to come in 1883.

British irregulars burning Zulu homesteads and carrying off cattle. Although the British were scrupulous in their treatment of non-combatants, Chelmsford sanctioned the destruction of Zulu homesteads and foodstores during the later stages of the war in a deliberate attempt to strike at the economic basis of support for Zulu resistance. (Private collection)

Renewed offensives

Despite the military victories in March and April, the prosecution of the campaign was becoming problematic for the British. In particular, the cost of the war was escalating, and the relationship between the civilian and military authorities in Natal was severely strained. The arrival of reinforcements created an inevitable demand for transport vehicles, while the easy pickings to be had working for the military began to disrupt the settler economy. The longer the war dragged on, the more exaggerated these problems became. Sir Henry Bulwer, moreover, was severely irritated by what he regarded as Chelmsford's high-handed attempts to wrest the control of colonial forces away from the civil power. The diversionary attacks mounted along the border to support the advance of the Eshowe relief column had often involved colonial troops, and when Bulwer objected to this Chelmsford overruled him. By April 1879, the relationship between the two had become almost unworkable.

This wrangle was not lost on the government in London, who in due course would send out an officer with full civil and military powers – Sir Garnet Wolseley – to supersede both Chelmsford and Frere, to resolve these issues and concentrate on bringing the war in the field to a successful conclusion.

Whatever problems the British faced at this stage of the war, they were infinitely worse for the Zulu. The losses at Khambula and Gingindlovu had been a severe blow, dispersing not only the concentrations in the coastal sector, but the king's main striking army as well. Within days, at opposite ends of the country, the Zulu had been scattered. The British now maintained effective control of the border on both sides of the Lower Thukela, and, despite their withdrawal from Eshowe, dominated the country for 20 miles (32km) inland. In the north, the abaQulusi – who had joined the main army in the attack on Khambula – had suffered heavily, and had been forced to abandon the Hlobane stronghold, which they had defended so successfully only the day before. The situation further deteriorated when, on 5 April, British troops from the Luneburg garrison intercepted a small party of Zulu raiders, and in the ensuing skirmish killed the redoubtable Prince Mbilini. The death of the most able guerrilla leader of the war left the Zulu hold over the northern districts distinctly fragile.

The mounting casualty toll, moreover, was beginning to undermine support for the war among the civilian population. When the *amabutho* dispersed and the men returned to their homes, the extent of the losses became fully apparent. British spies reported that the homesteads of Zululand seemed to be full of wounded men, and that mourning songs could be heard along the length of the border. In some areas, indeed, the civilian population had abandoned the country opposite the border altogether, since it was impossible to protect homesteads and livestock from British raids. Women, children and cattle were removed to inaccessible hills and caves which served as traditional places of refuge.

The king and his council saw in this ominous signs of defeat. The king had not wanted the war, but had sufficient confidence in his army to believe it might repel an initial attack. And indeed it had, although the lesson of Rorke's Drift was that it was acutely vulnerable in the face of a combination of secure defences and heavy firepower. The king had guessed that the British would also learn the lesson of this, and despite his orders to the contrary his army had proved him right at both

Khambula and Gingindlovu. Now Cetshwayo began to suspect a bitter truth: that the British resolve was undented, and that the longer the war went on, the less hope he had of winning it in the field. Furthermore, the British were making determined attempts to persuade the *amakhosi* to abandon their allegiance to the king, as Prince Hamu had done. While most remained conspicuously loyal, the pressure on them was sure to increase with each British victory.

As a result, the king attempted to open negotiations with the British in the hope of warding off a greater disaster. But the British rebuffed him; if Chelmsford and Frere had been unwilling to negotiate in the dark days after Isandlwana, they were even less so now, with the war shifting in their favour. Nothing but military subjugation, it seemed, would satisfy them.

This was a stance which committed the Zulu to further confrontations, for whatever doubts the high command now entertained about their ultimate success, ordinary Zulu in the *amabutho* remained defiant despite their losses. They regarded Khambula and Gingindlovu as aberrations, despising the British troops for their failure to fight fairly in the open, and convinced that they could achieve a further Isandlwana if only they could confront the British on similar terms.

The British, however, strove to avoid exactly that, and by May 1879 Lord Chelmsford had sufficient troops to begin a fresh invasion of Zululand.

Although he had learned the bitter lesson of stretching his resources too thinly, Chelmsford did not entirely abandon his old strategy. Although the Zulu army was clearly shaken by its defeats, he could not afford to ignore the possibility of a counter-attack. As a result, he retained the concept of invading on more than one front, but reduced his effective strength to two columns, although these were much stronger than those with which he'd taken to the field in January. One column, composed of Pearson's old command combined with the Eshowe relief column, and re-designated the 1st Division,

would advance through the coastal districts. Chelmsford intended that the 1st Division should play a largely supporting role, however, and rather than advance towards oNdini, it was to suppress local resistance, and establish a landing stage on an appropriate beach where supplies might be landed from the sea if necessary.

To make his advance on oNdini, Chelmsford created a new column, the 2nd Division. This was made up largely of reinforcements, fresh out from Britain, and it included a cavalry brigade, consisting of two regular cavalry regiments – the 1st (King's) Dragoon Guards and 17th Lancers – who had been sent out to compensate for Chelmsford's chronic shortage of cavalry. This column would advance in tandem with Wood's old left flank column, which was still based at Khambula, and which would retain a degree of independence under a new name, the Flying Column.

The combined 2nd Division/Flying Column would advance through central Zululand following a route which had originally been chosen for the old centre column. Chelmsford wished to spare his reinforcements the unnerving sight of Isandlwana, however – where the unburied British dead still lay on the ground – so he opted instead to begin the invasion north of Rorke's Drift. The 2nd Division would cut across country to effect a junction with the Flying Column, then together they would move south and – beyond Isandlwana – pick up the old track to oNdini.

Isandlwana could not be ignored entirely, however. Chelmsford was under considerable public pressure to bury the dead, and furthermore the transport wagons which had been abandoned on the field in January would be very necessary for use in the new invasion. As a result, on 21 May, the British made their first return to the battlefield, collecting together the serviceable wagons, and covering over some of the desiccated corpses which still lay strewn among the long grass.

Throughout May, the 2nd Division assembled at Landman's Drift on the Ncome, and British patrols pressed into Zululand,

As the British 1st Division began to occupy the coastal districts in overwhelming numbers, local Zulu *amakhosi* accepted the inevitability of defeat. Prince Magwendu kaMpande (centre) had fought at the battle of Isandlwana, but surrendered towards the end of April. (Private collection)

scouting out the road. The Zulu seemed to have abandoned that stretch of the border, concentrating instead in the hills 20 miles (32km) beyond. The new invasion began on 1 June when the 2nd Division crossed the border – and immediately disaster struck. A patrol of nine men, who had ridden ahead of the column, was ambushed in a deserted Zulu homestead on the banks of the Tshotshozi river. Four men were killed – one of them was an African scout, two were troopers in the irregular cavalry, and the fourth was Louis Napoleon Bonaparte, the exiled Prince Imperial of France.

A curious set of circumstances had brought the prince to Zululand. In 1848, after 30 years of exile from French politics, the Bonaparte family returned to power in France. The great Napoleon's nephew, Louis Napoleon, had ridden on a tide of revolutionary fervour all the way into the corridors of the Tuilieries palace. Louis had subsequently suspended democratic government, declared France an empire, and adopted the title Emperor Napoleon III. Under Napoleon III France once more became a world power, but in 1870 the emperor was manoeuvred into war by Bismarck of Prussia, and spectacularly defeated. The Second Empire collapsed, and the Imperial family sought refuge in Britain. Here the emperor died, and his young son – also called Louis – became the heir in exile to Bonapartist dreams of a restoration.

Deeply imbued with the family tradition of military glory, young Louis, the Prince Imperial, was allowed to train as a British officer, although protocol prevented him from taking a serving commission. When news of Isandlwana reached England, he begged to be allowed to go to Zululand, hoping to see real action in a war which could have no political repercussions in Europe. He was eventually allowed to go out as an observer, with no official standing, a celebrity tourist whom Chelmsford was asked to take under his wing.

The prince was given a post as ADC on Chelmsford's staff. He had taken part in several of the patrols of late May, and on a number of occasions had proved himself to be reckless. He had been confined to camp, but on 1 June had been allowed out, with only a small escort, in the belief that the advance of the column made any Zulu presence unlikely. It was the prince himself who had suggested resting at a Zulu homestead several miles ahead of the column; here the party was surprised by a group of Zulu scouts who had been watching British movements. The patrol scattered, Louis failed to mount his horse in the confusion, and was killed.

The Prince's body was recovered the following day and sent back to England for burial. The incident caused considerable interest in the British press – the patrol's surviving officer was court-martialled for abandoning the prince to his fate, but eventually released – but in truth it was a minor incident of the campaign. Such skirmishes were common as the war progressed, and it was only the prince's rank which added a particular poignancy to this one.

On 5 June, just a few days after the prince's death, cavalry from both columns dispersed a Zulu force which had assembled across the track at the eZungeni hills. For the most part, however, the Zulu were no longer

Louis Napoleon Bonaparte, the Prince Imperial of France. The prince accompanied British forces in an unofficial capacity, but habitually wore the undress uniform of a British artillery officer. This is one of a group of last photographs taken in Durban on his way to the front; his cropped hair makes him look older than his 23 years. (Private collection)

Second Invasion of Zululand

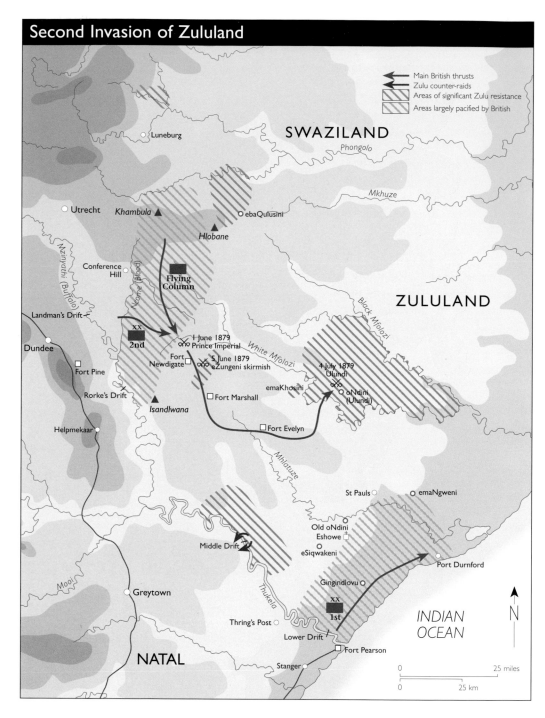

Main British thrusts
Zulu counter-raids
Areas of significant Zulu resistance
Areas largely pacified by British

SWAZILAND

Luneburg

Phongolo

Mkhuze

Utrecht   *Khambula* ▲

ebaQulusini ○

Hlobane ▲

Nzinyathi (Buffalo)

Conference Hill ○

Ncome (Blood)

Flying Column ■

ZULULAND

Black Mfolozi

Landman's Drift

Dundee ○

XX
2nd ■

Fort Pine □

Fort Newdigate □

1 June 1879
Prince Imperial

5 June 1879
eZungeni skirmish

White Mfolozi

emaKhosini ○

4 July 1879
Ulundi

oNdini (Ulundi) ○

Rorke's Drift ○

Isandlwana ▲

Fort Marshall □

Helpmekaar ○

Fort Evelyn □

Mhlatuze

St Pauls ○

emaNgweni ○

Mooi

Old oNdini ○
Eshowe □
eSiqwakeni ○

Middle Drift

Thukela

Gingindlovu ○

Port Durnford ○

Greytown ○

XX
1st ■

INDIAN
OCEAN

Thring's Post ○

Lower Drift

Fort Pearson □

NATAL

Stanger ○

N

0   25 miles

0   25 km

in a position to mount a challenge to the British advance so far away from oNdini. Although the king had reassembled his army, his strategy was to concentrate around the capital, to make one last attempt to defend the Zulu heartland. In the meantime, he

continued to send envoys to the British asking for peace terms – and the British continued to turn them away.

Indeed, Chelmsford's resolve to bring the war to a decisive conclusion was stiffened by the news that the British government had sent Sir Garnet Wolseley to South Africa to replace him. Wolseley did not arrive in Cape Town until 23 June, however, and by that stage Chelmsford was so deep into Zululand that it was impossible to control him. Wolseley hurried to Durban, and then attempted a short cut to the front by landing at Port Durnford, the beachhead established by the 1st Division. A heavy swell prevented him, however, and by the time he had returned to Durban and made his way overland, the war was all but over.

On 26 June, Chelmsford's column came within sight of the emaKhosini valley, on the south bank of the White Mfolozi river. This was the ancestral homeland of the Zulu people, where the great kings of the past were buried, and the valley contained a number of important royal homesteads. The

British sallied into the valley, setting fire to many of the homesteads; ironically, Zulu scouts preferred to burn the rest, rather than let them fall into British hands. The omens for the future of the Zulu Royal House were bleak.

At the beginning of July, the combined 2nd Division and Flying Column descended from the Mthonjaneni heights into the valley of the White Mfolozi. The homesteads surrounding oNdini were clearly visible across the river, as were the large numbers of Zulu who had been assembled there. Chelmsford's objectives were at last before him. Here, on the south bank of the river, he paused for a few days to prepare for the final confrontation, and here King Cetshwayo made one last desperate effort to open negotiations. This time, he was frustrated by his own warriors, for when the king sent a herd of his famous white cattle to the river as a peace offering, the young men of the uKhandempemvu regiment refused to let them pass. They would not allow the king to embarrass himself, they said, for they were not yet defeated.

One of a number of heroic images of the prince's death which appeared in the British illustrated papers. This one is broadly accurate in the way in which it depicts Louis turning to face his attackers in the bottom of the donga, *but in fact his sword had dropped from his scabbard during the rush from the homestead. (Private collection)*

Then, on 3 July, Chelmsford sent his irregulars across the river to scout for a suitable place for a battle. The irregulars were ambushed by Zulu hiding in the long grass and chased from the field, but they had achieved their objective. At dawn the following morning, leaving only a small detachment to guard his baggage train, Lord Chelmsford crossed the White Mfolozi at the head of the largest concentration of British troops yet fielded in South Africa – over 4,000 white troops, including the 17th Lancers, 1,000 auxiliaries, 12 field guns, and two hand-cranked Gatling machine-guns.

Once they reached the undulating country beyond, Chelmsford formed his troops into a square, the infantry four ranks deep, with artillery pieces distributed at the corners and sides. As this cumbersome formation slowly manoeuvred towards the

selected spot, the irregular cavalry were sent out to search for the Zulus. The square took up a position on a low rise close to the homestead of kwaNodwengu, the guns unlimbered and the infantry faced outwards, two ranks kneeling. By this time, the Zulu had begun to emerge from the surrounding homesteads, or from sheltered gulleys where they had bivouacked. Ironically, they too had chosen this spot for the final

confrontation of the war, convinced that if they could surround the British there, they could defeat them. The irregulars retired inside the infantry lines, the Zulu advanced – and the battle known to the British as Ulundi began.

For perhaps 45 minutes the Zulu attacked the square on all sides. In particular, they made a determined attack on the right rear, rushing up to within 30 or 40 yards before being shot down. Yet the zone of fire created by the British around their square was impenetrable, and some Zulu regiments, discouraged by their losses earlier in the war, hung back. When they showed the first signs of retreat, Chelmsford ordered his Lancers to chase them from the field. The 17th emerged from the square, dressed their lines, and charged, cutting a great swathe through the retreating warriors. The irregulars followed behind them, shooting down Zulu survivors. Once the main Zulu forces had gone, shelled until they had retired over the hills and out of sight, the auxiliaries of the NNC were sent out to finish off the wounded. For both sides, the Anglo-Zulu War remained a struggle without prisoners until the very end.

Once the battle was won, Chelmsford ordered the cavalry to set fire to the great circles of huts which constituted the royal homestead. By late afternoon, Chelmsford had returned to his camp across the river. He had lost just two officers and ten men killed, one officer mortally wounded and a further 69 men wounded.

By contrast, well over 1,000 Zulu bodies lay in the long grass surrounding the British position, and the burning royal homestead would smoulder for several days.

In a stroke, the British had reduced the heart of Zululand to ashes and blood.

Zulu envoys, carrying elephant tusks as a gesture of good-will, enter Lord Chelmsford's camp during the final advance on oNdini. In fact, the tide of war had irrevocably turned in favour of the British, and King Cetshwayo's peace overtures were consistently rebuffed. (Private collection)

Pacifying Zululand

Lord Chemsford wasted no time in withdrawing from central Zululand, and on the day after the battle the 2nd Division and Flying Column began to retire from the White Mfolozi valley. For Chelmsford, the battle was a personal vindication which wiped out the air of defeat which had hung about him since January. His honour restored, he was only too happy to resign his command, and leave Wolseley to whatever remained of the war. Indeed, Lord Chelmsford returned to Britain as the victor of Ulundi rather than the vanquished of Isandlwana, and the Victorian establishment rallied round to support him. He was showered with awards and honorary appointments – but it is perhaps significant that he never commanded an army in the field again.

Lord Wolseley was irritated by Chelmsford's actions. He had tried repeatedly to delay the final British advance so that he could reach the front to take command, but he had been cheated of the final victory. Moreover, Wolseley felt that Chelmsford's withdrawal was premature, that the Zulu were not yet completely defeated, and that by retiring so soon Chelmsford had sent the wrong moral message.

To some degree, he was right. Large portions of Zululand had been untouched by the British presence, and Chelmsford had made no effort to secure the person of King Cetshwayo himself. The king had not stayed

The final battle of the war, known to the British as the battle of Ulundi. The British square was impenetrable to Zulu attacks, and once the Zulu assaults began to falter, the British infantry marched aside (right) to allow the cavalry to emerge – and chase the Zulu from the field. (Private collection)

Battle of Ulundi, 4 July 1879

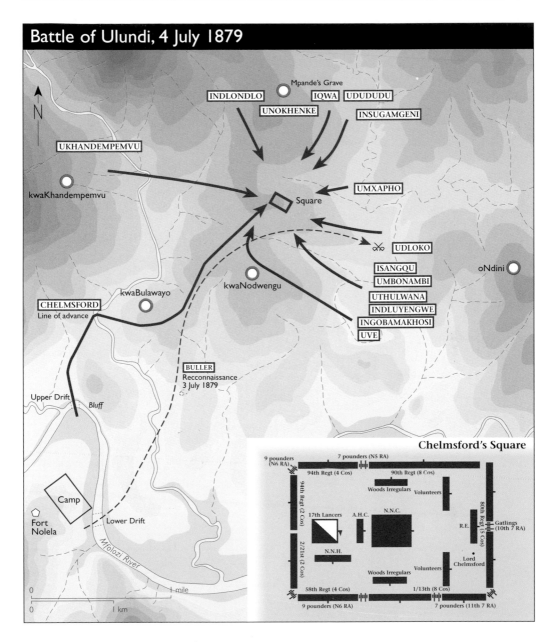

to watch the final humiliation of his army, but had listened to the sounds of battle from the hills north of oNdini. When his defeat was obvious, he had retired into the territory of his great councillor, Mnyamana Buthelezi, accompanied only by his personal attendants. From here he attempted to negotiate with the British for his surrender. After the battle, most of the royal *amabutho* had dispersed, the men simply returning to their homes.

Yet in fact, as Chelmsford had correctly assumed, the defeat at oNdini had knocked the last of the fight out of the Zulu. When Cetshwayo subsequently ordered some of his younger regiments to assemble to build him a new royal homestead, beyond the reach of the British, they refused to do so. In the coastal districts, even before oNdini, the 1st Division had destroyed a number of important royal homesteads without even a token of resistance from the Zulu. Indeed,

Once the battle of Ulundi was won, Chelmsford allowed his officers to explore the royal homestead at oNdini, before setting it ablaze. Here troops watch as a European-style dwelling, in the centre of the king's personal quarters, goes up in smoke. (Private collection)

the British had occupied the area in such numbers that a number of local *amakhosi* had finally accepted the inevitable, and begun to surrender. This process accelerated once news of the battle became known.

Wolseley, however, was determined that the Zulu should be fully subjugated, so once Chelmsford had left the country, he reorganised the British forces. Some units were allowed to go home, but others were formed into two new columns. The old Flying Column was placed under the command of Lieutenant Colonel Baker Russell, while a new column was formed out of the 1st Division, and given to the command of Lieutenant Colonel Clarke. Both columns were by that time in the east of the country, and Baker Russell was ordered to march back through the centre of the country towards Wood's old base at Khambula. Along the way, he was to

Perhaps the most historic photograph taken during the war; the view from the British camp on the White Mfolozi on 4 July, looking towards the smoke rising from the Ulundi battlefield, with oNdini itself burning to the right. (Private collection)

intimidate any Zulu groups who might still be inclined to resist. Wolseley himself, accompanied by Clarke's column, decided to reoccupy oNdini.

Wolseley established a new camp within sight of the ruins of oNdini on 10 August. From here he insisted that Zulu *amakhosi* and *izinduna* who had not yet surrendered should come to him to submit. From here, too, he sent out patrols to try to capture King Cetshwayo.

The British embarked on the hunt for the king with an enthusiasm for the chase born of a realisation that, for them, this would be the last great adventure of the war. Cavalry patrols were sent north into sparsely populated bush country along the banks of the Black Mfolozi river, and vied with each other to find him. For the most part, despite the war-weariness which prevailed, ordinary Zulus still refused to betray him. Eventually, however, Cetshwayo was captured at the remote kwaDwasa homestead in the Ngome forest in northern Zululand by a party of Dragoons led by Major Richard Marter.

King Cetshwayo was taken to Wolseley's camp at oNdini, where he was told that the

British had decided to depose and exile him. He was then sent to the coast where he was taken on board a steamer, and set sail for Cape Town.

Sir Garnet had already disposed of his kingdom. Ironically, the British government had already turned its back on the Confederation policy which had provoked the war. Confederation had died, along with so many others, on the field of Isandlwana, and Frere's policies were discredited. A change of administration in London, from expansionist Conservative to cautious Liberal, meant that there was no will in Britain to support an expensive occupation of Zululand. Wolseley's instructions had been to impose a peace settlement which would reduce the danger a unified Zululand might pose to British interests, while at the same time avoiding the expense and commitment of outright annexation.

Wolseley's solution was a classic case of divide and rule. The country was to be split among 13 chiefs appointed by the British. The criteria by which these chiefs were selected depended on their sympathy towards the British cause, or their hostility towards the Royal House. At least two were high-ranking members of the old establishment who had deserted the king during the war, to fight for the British – Prince Hamu kaNzibe, and Cetshwayo's erstwhile white councillor, John Dunn. One of the new appointees was an African outsider who had also fought for the British. Others included representatives of old chiefdoms within the country – in the belief that pre-Shakan Zululand could somehow be restored – or men such as Zibhebhu kaMapitha, a former Zulu general and *inkhosi* of the Mandlakazi section, who had displayed a markedly independent attitude.

On 1 September Wolseley called a meeting of the great chiefs at oNdini, and informed them of his settlement. Three days later, he left oNdini, and on the 5th Clarke's column began to withdraw, retiring across country, by way of the old Middle Drift, so as to intimidate the powerful border chiefdoms there who had been reluctant to submit. Meanwhile, Baker Russell's column had reached northern Zululand where a few recalcitrant followers of the late Prince

On 28 August King Cetshwayo was finally captured by British Dragoons at a small homestead in the Ngome forest, where he had taken refuge. He was taken to the coast, and sent into exile at the Cape. (Cardiff Castle Museum)

Mbilini still refused to surrender. For several days in the first week of September, Russell's men attempted to drive a handful of Zulus out of the caves where they had taken refuge, and it was here that the last shots of the war were fired. Eventually, the British lost patience, and blew up the mouths of the caves with the last stragglers still inside.

For the British, the Zulu War was over. Wolseley lost no time in moving on to the next problem – he travelled straight to the Transvaal, where the Pedi paramount, King Sekhukhune, had been defying Boer authority since before the annexation. On 20 November, a British force consisting of units that had served just a few months before in Zululand, supported by a large army supplied by the Swazi king, overran and defeated King Sekhukhune's followers at his royal homestead.

For many in the professional British military, the war had marked just one adventurous episode in what often proved to be long and varied careers. The battalions moved on to new postings, to garrison duty elsewhere in the Empire, or, if they were lucky, a return home. Many of the officers went on to serve in the much larger British campaigns in Egypt and the Sudan, and some of those who were lieutenants or captains in 1879 returned to South Africa in 1899 to fight against a very different enemy – the Boers – as generals. For some, it was a doleful experience, and the fate of Redvers Buller perhaps epitomises them all. A dynamic lieutenant colonel in 1879 – he won his Victoria Cross at Hlobane – he proved himself too inflexible to cope easily with the challenges of Boer warfare, and his early failures to relieve Ladysmith left an indelible stain on his reputation. Yet in truth, there were few long-term military lessons to be learned from the Anglo-Zulu War, apart from one delivered acerbically by the satirical magazine *Punch* – 'despise not your enemy'. For the British, most colonial wars were unique in the challenges they posed, a product of particular enemy skills and a distinct environment, and the Anglo-Zulu War was no exception. It was, in a

sense, part of an age of warfare which was already passing, for with the spread of improved weapons worldwide, fewer and fewer campaigns would be won by standing shoulder to shoulder in the same formations which had defeated Napoleon. The famous red coat, which had come to symbolise so much of the growth of the British Empire, would still sometimes appear on the battlefield for a decade to come, but would never again be worn in action in such numbers as it was in Zululand.

Politically, the defeat of the two most powerful African kingdoms in eastern South Africa – the Zulu and the Pedi – did little to further British domination of the area. The Transvaal Boers, who had never reconciled themselves to British rule, now no longer felt the need for British protection against their African neighbours. In December 1880 – when most of the troops assembled for the Zulu campaign had left the region – the Boers rebelled. British garrisons around the country were besieged, and a British column marching to secure Pretoria was shot to pieces. Troops were hastily assembled in Natal to march to their relief, but the Boers blocked the road at the Laing's Nek pass, in the Kahlamba mountains. British attempts in early 1881 to break the Boer lines led to two defeats – Laing's Nek and Schuinshoogte (Ingogo) – followed by a crowning disaster at Majuba hill. The British general, Sir George Colley, attempted to outflank the Boer position, only to find himself trapped on the mountain-top. Colley was killed and his command routed, and in the aftermath the British government lost the political will to regain control of the Transvaal. Ironically, this was the very aim King Cetshwayo had striven to achieve in the Zulu War – but the Boers' white skins made it much easier for the British to acknowledge defeat at their hands. The Transvaal was returned to Boer rule, with the British maintaining only vague rights to suzerainty – an unsatisfactory situation which would itself become a cause of later Anglo-Boer conflicts.

It was the Zulu people who suffered most from the British invasion, however. It is almost impossible to obtain an accurate

Inkhosi Zibhebhu kaMapitha, head of the Mandlakazi – a collateral section of the Royal House which dominated northern Zululand. Zibhebhu had proved an able general in 1879, but because of his pro-western outlook he was appointed by the British as one of the 13 chiefs set to rule Zululand after the war was over. He became the leader of the anti-royalist faction, and defeated King Cetshwayo in the bitter civil war of 1883. (Pietermaritzburg Archives Depot)

figure for losses during the war, but it was in the region of 10,000 – young men who were not full-time soldiers, and whose loss was keenly felt in the community at large. The great centres of royal authority were destroyed, along with hundreds of ordinary family homesteads, while the British had carried away thousands of cattle which belonged not only to the royal herds, but to ordinary Zulus alike. Many of the chiefs appointed by the British were deeply unpopular with the people over whom they ruled, and surviving members of the extensive Royal House retained widespread loyalty. Yet the representatives of the new order were keenly sensitive to any expression of royalist sympathies, and within a year of the British withdrawal royalists began to complain that they were being oppressed.

The British settlement, however, offered them no redress. When a group of royalists walked to the colonial capital at Pietermaritzburg to appeal for a more just settlement, they were refused, and indeed British colonial policy remained firmly opposed to the aspirations of the Royal House. Most colonial officials regarded the royal family as the root of ant-British sentiment in Zululand, a stance which only increased royalist frustration and led to tension and violence.

King Cetshwayo himself was placed in genteel captivity at the old castle in Cape Town. From here, once he had recovered from

the shock of his defeat, he began to seek to influence Zulu affairs from a distance. It became fashionable for wealthy travellers to visit him, and his dignity and the apparent injustice of the war began to win sympathy in influential circles in Britain. By 1882, repression and revenge were endemic in Zululand, and the Colonial Office was beginning to ponder the effectiveness of Wolseley's settlement. In 1882, King Cetshwayo was allowed to visit London to argue his case for restoration. The king became a popular figure with the London crowds; having tamed the fearsome ogre depicted in the illustrated papers at the time of Isandlwana, the British public was delighted to find he was actually an imposing and regal figure smartly dressed in European clothes.

The British decided to restore Cetshwayo to part of his old kingdom. A considerable portion of northern Zululand was set aside to be ruled over by the most ardent anti-royalists, chiefly Prince Hamu and *inkhosi* Zibhebhu. Part of southern Zululand was taken over as a British Reserve, to be administered by a Resident. The king was therefore left with only the middle part of his old territory, and he was furthermore prevented from restoring the military system.

The king returned to Zululand in January 1883, and settled again at oNdini, building a new royal homestead close by the ruins of the old. The British refusal to allow him to revive the *amabutho* system undermined his ability to control his followers. The bonds which bound young Zulus to serve the king were broken, and there were in any case no *amakhanda* left to house the warriors, and no royal herds to sustain them. Many Zulu who remained loyal to the king still recognised their allegiance to their old *amabutho*, and were still prepared to answer the king's call, but the regiments were a shadow of their former selves. Indeed, many warriors in the coming struggles, whatever their allegiance, preferred to muster and fight under their local chiefs rather than in the royal regiments – an indication of the extent to which the British invasion had destroyed much of the apparatus of central control.

Indeed, in many ways Cetshwayo's restoration came too late to save Zululand. The divisions engendered by the British invasion had intensified to such a degree that Cetshwayo's return merely inflamed the violence. Royalist supporters, acting on their own initiative, sought to revenge themselves on their most implacable enemy, *inkhosi* Zibhebhu. But Zibhebhu defeated them at the battle of Msebe in March, and gathered his own forces for a counter-attack. In July he made a sudden move across the Black Mfolozi and struck at oNdini itself. The attack coincided with a gathering of prominent royalist *amakhosi* and warriors at oNdini, but the speed of Zibhebhu's advance took them by surprise. The royalists, many of them assembled in their old pre-war *amabutho*, went forward in some confusion to meet Zibhebhu, but were easily routed. Cetshwayo himself only just managed to escape, while over 50 notables – heads of lineages dating back to King Shaka's time, councillors, generals and royal officials who constituted the establishment of the old kingdom – were run down and killed.

In many respects, the battle of oNdini in 1883 marks the true destruction of the old Zulu order, the end of a process which the British had begun four years before. The civil war was a direct product of the tensions unleashed by the British invasion, and by the failure of the British to invest in a lasting settlement. The invasion had successfully turned Zulu against Zulu, and in the end the civil war utterly shattered the royalist infrastructure as the invasion itself had never done.

King Cetshwayo fled to the protection of the British Resident at Eshowe. Here he died on 8 February 1884, ostensibly from a heart attack.

The king's death did not halt the bloodshed. His son, Prince Dinuzulu, assumed leadership of the royalist cause, and appealed to the Transvaal Boers to intervene. In 1884 a combined royalist and Boer army defeated Zibhebhu at the battle of Tshaneni. Yet the price to be paid was again high: the Boers demanded land in reward, and nearly a third of Zululand was marked out to Boer farmers. Prince Dinuzulu objected, and the British government intervened – worried more by the prospect of a Boer republic gaining access to the sea, and the influence of rival European empires, than by the plight of the Zulu. In 1887 Britain at last annexed Zululand; Dinuzulu rebelled, and for the last time British redcoats fought against Zulu warriors in the green hills of Zululand. But the rebellion of 1888 was a minor affair, undistinguished by further Isandlwanas or Rorke's Drifts, and Prince Dinuzulu at last surrendered. He was exiled to St Helena.

The royalist defeat in 1888 paved the way for the subjugation and exploitation of the Zulu people and their land. Over the next 20 years, Zululand was opened up for white settlement, and the colonial administration of Natal was extended across Zululand. The

ABOVE The battle of oNdini, 21 July 1883; Zibhebhu's victorious Mandlakazi rout the king's supporters as the royal homestead burns. The battle was the logical conclusion of the division settlement imposed by the British, and marked the true end of the old Zulu order. (Private collection)

BELOW The body of King Cetshwayo, lying in state, prepared for burial, at Eshowe, February 1884. The restoration of the king had proved a personal and national tragedy. (Private collection)

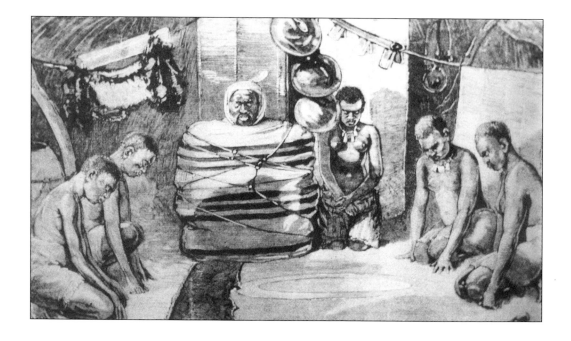

area would be touched by violence one last time when in 1906, African groups living in Natal rebelled against the steady reduction of their lands, power and wealth which had characterised their experience of white rule. The rebels fled to Zululand, and tried to harness the potent symbolism of the old Zulu to spread the rebellion, using King Cetshwayo's grave as a rallying point. But only a few Zulu chiefs joined them, and the rebellion was ruthlessly crushed by colonial troops armed with Maxim machine-guns and quick-firing artillery.

In retrospect, the Anglo-Zulu War emerges as part of a broader pattern of the reduction of the indigenous political systems of Africans in South Africa, a process that had begun as soon as the first Europeans arrived at the Cape in the 17th century, and which continued into the 20th century. What makes it stand out from the flow of history is the intensity of the Zulu resistance – which has in some respects come to symbolise that common struggle – the shock that resistance inflicted on the British, and the brutality of the fighting that followed as a result. For the Zulu people, the legacy of that resistance has remained an uncomfortable one.

Although this photograph dates from a later conflict – the 1906 rebellion – it depicts a scene all too common to the battlefields of 1879; a Zulu senior lies dead beside his great war-shield. The price paid by the Zulu for their resistance to colonial encroachment was indeed a heavy one. (Local History Museums, Durban)

Further reading

Primary sources

Contemporary memoirs, or modern compilations of first-hand accounts:

Bennett, Lt. Col. I.H.W., *Eyewitness in Zululand: The Campaign Reminiscences of Colonel W.A. Dunne*, London, 1989.

Child, D. (ed.), *The Zulu War Journal of Colonel Henry Harford*, Pietermaritzburg, 1978.

Clarke, S. (ed.), *Invasion of Zululand, 1879*, Houghton, 1979.

Clarke S. (ed.), *Zululand at War*, Houghton, 1984.

Emery, F., *The Red Soldier: Letters from the Zulu War 1879*, London, 1977.

Filter, H. (comp.) and Bouquin, S. (trans.), *Paulina Dlamini: Servant of Two Kings*, Durban, 1986.

Greaves, A. and Best, B., *The Curling Letters of the Zulu War*, Barnsley, 2001.

Hamilton-Browne, Col. G.A., *Lost Legionary in South Africa*, London, 1913 (?)

Hart-Synot, B.M. (ed.), *Letters of Major-General Fitzroy Hart-Synot*, London, 1912.

Knight, I., *'By the Orders of the Great White Queen': Campaigning in Zululand through the Eyes of the British Soldier*, London, 1992.

Laband, J., *Fight Us in the Open: The Anglo-Zulu War through Zulu Eyes*, Pietermaritzburg, 1985.

Laband, J., *Lord Chelmsford's Zululand Campaign*, Stroud, 1994.

Mackinnon, J.P. and Shadbolt, S. (comps), *The South Africa Campaign 1879*, London, 1882.

Mitford, B., *Through the Zulu Country: Its Battlefields and its People*, London, 1883.

Molyneux, Maj.-Gen. W.C.F., *Campaigning in South Africa and Egypt*, London, 1896.

Mossop, G., *Running the Gauntlet*, London, 1937.

Norris-Newman, C.L., *In Zululand with the British throughout the War of 1879*, London, 1880.

Parr, Capt. H. Hallam, *A Sketch of the Kaffir and Zulu Wars*, London, 1880.

Vijn, C. (translated and edited by the Rt. Rev. J.W. Colenso), *Cetshwayo's Dutchman*, London, 1880.

Webb, C. de B. (ed.), *A Zulu Boy's Recollections of the Zulu War*, Natalia magazine, December 1978.

Webb, C. de B. and Wright, J.B. (eds), *A Zulu King Speaks: Statements Made by Cetshwayo kaMpande on the History and Customs of His People*, Pietermaritzburg, 1978.

Whitehouse, H. (ed.), *A Widow-Making War: The Life and Death of a British Officer in Zululand 1879*, Nuneaton, 1995.

Wood, Sir H.E., *From Midshipman to Field Marshal*, London, 1906.

Secondary sources:

Binns, C.T., *The Last Zulu King*, London, 1963.

Castle, I. and Knight, I., *Fearful Hard Times: The Siege and Relief of Eshowe, 1879*, London, 1994.

Cope, R., *Ploughshare of War: The Origins of the Anglo-Zulu War, 1879*, Pietermaritzburg, 1999.

Drooglever, R.W.F., *The Road to Isandlwana: Colonel Anthony Durnford in Natal and Zululand*, London, 1992.

Gon, P., *The Road to Isandlwana: The Years of an Imperial Battalion*, Johannesburg, 1979.

Guy, J., *The Destruction of the Zulu Kingdom: The Civil War in Zululand, 1879–1884*, London, 1979.

Knight, I., *Brave Men's Blood: The Epic of the Zulu War, 1879*, London, 1990.

Knight, I., *Zulu: Isandlwana and Rorke's Drift*, London, 1992.

Knight, I., *Nothing Remains But to Fight: The Defence of Rorke's Drift*, London, 1993.

Knight, I., *The Anatomy of the Zulu Army: From Shaka to Cetshwayo*, London, 1995.

Knight, I., *With His Face to the Foe: The Life and Death of the Prince Imperial*, Staplehurst, 2001.

Knight, I., *The National Army Museum Book of the Zulu War*, London, 2003.

Knight, I. and Castle, I., *The Zulu War: Then and Now*, London, 1993.

Laband, J., *Rope of Sand: The Rise and Fall of the Zulu Kingdom in the Nineteenth Century*, Johannesburg, 1995 (published in the UK and US under the title *The Rise and Fall of the Zulu Nation*).

Laband, J., *The Atlas of the Later Zulu Wars, 1883–1888*, Pietermaritzburg, 2001.

Laband, J. and Thompson, P., *The Illustrated Guide to the Anglo-Zulu War*, Pietermaritzburg, 2000.

Laband, J., *The Atlas of the Later Zulu Wars, 1883–1888*, Pietermaritzburg 2001.

Index

abaQulusi 29, 43, 44, 47, 49, 51, 52, 74
Aborigines Protection Society 66
Afghan War, Second 8, 66–7
Afrikaners, nationalism 8
amabutho 12, 24
amahawur (shields) 23, 24
amakhanda (homesteads) 24
amakhosi (chiefs) 11
amaXhosa 16, 21, 26

Baker Russell, Lieutenant Colonel 85, 86–7
BaSotho 'Gun War' (1880–81) 65
'Basutos' 62, **62–3**
Boer War (1899–1902) 8, 67
Boers
    reaction to Zulu War 67–8
    rebellion (1880) 87
    settlement in KwaZulu-Natal 14, 15–16
Bonaparte, Louis Napoleon 63–4, 67, 76–7, **77**, **79**
Booth, Sergeant 44, 46
Border Levies 47
British Army
    1st Division 75, **76**, 79, 83, 85
    2nd Division 75, 76, 79, 82
    'Africa school' 67
    auxiliary forces 21–2, 61, **62–3**
    character 19
    communications 42, 43
    Flying Column 75, 79, 82, 85
    'India school' 67
    infantry battalions 19–20, **20**
    logistics 22, **22**
    strength 20–1
    uniform and equipment 19–20
Bromhead, Lieutenant Gonville 33, **38**
Buller, Lieutenant Colonel Redvers **49**
    and Boer War 87
    at Hlobane 49, 51, 52, 62, 87
    at Ulundi 64
Bulwer, Sir Henry
    and border raids 47, 74
    mediation policy 17
    and NNC 21

Campbell, Captain 51
Cape Frontier War 26
Cape of Good Hope 12
casualties 7, 38, 46, 54, 57, 74, 81, 87–8
Cetshwayo kaMpande **7**
    after Isandlwana and Rorke's Drift 40
    and Boer settlement 16
    burial **90**
    captivity 88
    capture of 85–6, **86**
    death 89
    and Hamu 43
    peace overtures 75, 78, 79, 83
    restoration of 89
    strategy 27, 47, 49, 74–5
    visit to London 88
Chard, Lieutenant John 33, 37, **37**, 38
Chelmsford, Lieutenant General Lord **20**
    and border raids 47, 74
    Eshowe, relief of 55, 57
    and Isandlwana 31–2, 38
    and Natal contingents 20–1
    oNdini, attack on 75, 80–1
    reputation 82

Zulu homesteads, destruction of 69
Zululand, first invasion of (January 1879) 26, 28
Zululand, second invasion of (May 1879) 75, **78**
Clarke, Lieutenant Colonel 85, 86
Cochrane, Captain William Francis Dundonald 58–65, **60**
Colenso, Bishop John 66
Colley, Sir George 87
Confederation policy 8, 15, 16, 68, 86

Dabulamanzi kaMpande 33, **36**, 56, 57
Dartnell, Major 31, 32
Delagoa Bay 11
Derby, Transvaal 44
diamonds, discovery of 15
Dinuzulu 89
Disraeli, Benjamin 66
dongas (erosion gulleys) 32–3, 61
Dunn, John 86
Durnford, Colonel Anthony 32, 33, 59–61, 70

Edendale Christian contingent 61, 64
Egypt 66
emaKhosini valley 79
Eshowe 30, 31, **34**, 43
    campaign (January–April 1879) **42**
    fieldwork 41
    relief of 47, 55, 57
eZungeni 72, 77

Farewell, Francis 12
farmhouses **16**
Fort Thinta 29
Frere, Sir Henry Bartle **15**
    Confederation policy 8, 15, 16
    criticisms of 68
    description of the Zulu 24
    and war with the Zulu 16–17, 18

Gingindlovu, battle of (2 April 1879) 55–7, **57**, **58–9**
Gladstone, William Ewart 67, 68
Glyn, Colonel Richard 28, 40
Godide kaNdlela 29, 30
Greytown, defences **40**

Hackett, Major Robert 53
Hamu kaNzibe 43–4, 75, 86, 89
Harford, Lieutenant Henry 59
Harward, Lieutenant 44, 46
heliograph equipment 41, 43
Helpmekaar 61
Hlobane mountain 47, **51**
    British attack on (28 March 1879) 49, 51–2, 72
Hlubi's Sotho detachment 61, 64

imizi (homesteads) 11
India 66
Isandlwana, battle of (22 January 1879) 7, 8, 31–3, **35**, 61, 66, 70
    battlefield today **32**
izimpondo zankomo ('the beasts' horns') 25
izinduna (state officials) 24

Kahlamba (Dragon Mountains) 11, 15
Khambula 40, 43
    battle of (29 March 1879) 52–5, **54–5**, 62, 72
kwaDwasa homestead 85
kwaGingindlovu 30, 55
    see also Gingindlovu, battle of

kwaNodwengu 81

Laing's Nek pass 87
Landman's Drift 75
Langalibalele rebellion (1873) 15
Lee, Bishop A.W. 8
Lower Thukela Drift
    British crossing at 26
    British ultimatum at (11 December 1878) 18, **18**
Luneburg 18, 26, 44, 72

Mafunzi **48**
Magwendu kaMpande **76**
Mahubulwana kaDumisela **48**
Maiwand, battle of (July 1880) 67
Majuba hill 87
Malakatha mountain 69
Mandlakazi 86
Mangeni river gorge 31
Manzimnyama stream 33
Marter, Major Richard 85
Martini-Henry rifles 20
Mavumengwana kaNdlela 29, 56
Mbilini waMswati **45**
    death 74
    and Luneburg raid 18, 44, 72
    at Ntombe drift 46, 47
    at Zungweni mountain 29–30
Mehlokazulu 73
Mfolozi rivers 11–12, 29, 64, 79, 85
Middle Drift 47, 60, 86
missionaries **13**
Mkhumbane stream 11
Mnyamana Buthelezi 52, 54, 83
Moriarty, Captain David 44
Mpande kaSenzangakhona 15
Msebe, battle of (March 1883) 89
Mthethwa 12
Mthonjaneni heights 72, 79
Muziwento 69
Mzinyathi river 14, 33

Natal 14–15
    rebellion (1906) 91
Natal Mounted Police (NMP) 21, 31
Natal Native Contingent (NNC) 21–2, **21**, 30, 31, 33,
    57, 81
Ncome river 26, 75
Ndwandwe 12
Ngome forest 85
Ngwebeni stream 32
Ntendeka hill 49, 52, 62
Ntombe, battle of (12 March 1879) 44, 46, **46**
Ntshingwayo kaMahole 28–9, **29**, 31, 47
Nyezane, battle of (22 January 1879) 30–1, **31**

oNdini (Zulu capital) 17, 26
    battle of (21 July 1883) 89, **90**
    British advance on 75, 80–1
    burning of **84, 85**

Pearson, Colonel Charles 30, **30**, 41, 43, 57
Pedi 16, 67, 87
Pietermaritzburg 40
Port Dunford 79
Port Natal 12, 13, 14
Pulleine, Lieutenant Colonel Henry 32, 33, 61

Rorke, James 33
Rorke's Drift
    battle of (23/24 January 1879) 7, 33–4, 37–8, **34, 39,**
        70, 72
    British crossing at 26, 28
Rowlands, Colonel 44, 68
Royal Engineers 33, 37
Russell, Colonel 49, 52, 62

Schuinshoogte (Ingogo) 87

Sekhukhune, King 87
Shaka kaSenzangakhona 12, 22, 24
Shepstone, George 70
'Shepstone's Horse' **64–5**
Shiyane hill 34, 37
Sihayo kaXongo 17, 18, 28, 69, 72
Siphezi mountain 69
Smith-Dorrien, Lieutenant Horace 59
Somopho kaZikhala 56, **56**
Sotho 16
South Africa
    British interests in 12
    situation in the 1870s **14**
Suez Canal 66
Swazi kingdom 18, 26, 67
    warriors **43**
Swedish missionary society 33

Thukela river 12, 14, 74
Thukela garrison 41
Transvaal, British annexation of 15
Tshaneni, battle of (1884) 89
Tshotshozi river 63
Twentyman, Major 47

uKhandempemvu regiment 73, 79
Ulundi, battle of (4 July 1879) 64, **64–5**, 72, 81, 82, **82,**
    83, 85
uThulwana 70, 72
Utrecht, Transvaal 26
Uys, Piet 52

Weatherley, Colonel 52
Williams, Lieutenant Charles 59
Wolseley, Sir Garnet 74, 79, 82, 85, 86, 87
Wombane 30
Wood, Colonel Henry Evelyn **28**
    and abaQulusi 43
    at Hlobane 47, 49, 51, 52, 53, 61–2
    at Khambula 41
    Ncome river, crossing of 26
    Zungweni mountain, attack on 29–30

Zibhebhu kaMapitha 33, 86, **88**, 89
Zulu
    and the British 13–14, 15, 16
    civilians **70, 71**
    guilds 22, 24
    homesteads, destruction of 69, **73**
    marriage 24, **25**
    rise of 11–12
Zulu army
    character and organisation 22, 24
    movement 25
    regalia **23**, 24
    tactics 24–5
    weapons 24–5
A Zulu Boy's Recollections of the Zulu War 69
Zulu War (1879)
    African reaction to 67–8
    British reaction to 66–7
    casualties 7, 38, 46, 54, 57, 74, 81, 87–8
    French reaction to 67
    lessons learned from 87
    Zulu reaction to 69–73
Zululand
    annexation of (1887) 89
    British interests in 12–13
    British invasion of (January 1879) 26–7, **27**
    British invasion of (May 1879) 75, **78**
    civil war 89
    conflicts within 11–12
    division of after the war 86
    geography 11
    society 11
    war in the north **50**
Zungweni mountain 29

Related titles from Osprey Publishing

CAMPAIGN (CAM)

**Strategies, tactics and battle experiences
of opposing armies**

0850459613 CAM 006 BALACLAVA 1854
1855321653 CAM 014 ZULU WAR 1879
1855322862 CAM 021 GRAVELOTTE-ST-PRIVAT 1870
185532301X CAM 023 KHARTOUM 1885
1855323338 CAM 027 TEL-EL-KEBIR 1882
1855323605 CAM 028 NEW ORLEANS 1815
1855323680 CAM 029 OMDURMAN 1898
1855324660 CAM 038 COLENSO 1899
185532458X CAM 039 LITTLE BIG HORN 1876
1855325063 CAM 041 RORKE'S DRIFT 1879
1855325039 CAM 045 MAJUBA 1881
1855326183 CAM 051 INKERMAN 1854
1855327015 CAM 057 SAN JUAN HILL 1898
1841761818 CAM 085 PEKING 1900
1841760900 CAM 089 THE ALAMO 1836

NEW VANGUARD (NVG)

**Design, development and operation
of the machinery of war**

Contact us for more details – see below

WARRIOR (WAR)

**Motivation, training, combat experiences
and equipment of individual soldiers**

1855323192 WAR 004 US CAVALRYMAN 1865–90
1855324741 WAR 014 ZULU 1816–1906

ELITE (ELI)

**Uniforms, equipment, tactics and personalities
of troops and commanders**

0850458641 ELI 021 THE ZULUS
1855321092 ELI 032 BRITISH FORCES IN ZULULAND 1879
1855321556 ELI 036 THE TEXAS RANGERS
1841760544 ELI 071 QUEEN VICTORIA'S COMMANDERS

ESSENTIAL HISTORIES (ESS)

**Concise overviews of major wars
and theatres of war**

1841761869 ESS 002 THE CRIMEAN WAR
1841763969 ESS 052 THE BOER WAR 1899–1902

FORTRESS (FOR)

**Design, technology and history
of key fortresses, strategic positions
and defensive systems**

Contact us for more details – see below

MEN-AT-ARMS (MAA)

**Uniforms, equipment, history
and organisation of troops**

0850452562 MAA 057 THE ZULU WAR
0850452546 MAA 059 THE SUDAN CAMPAIGNS 1881–98
0850450497 MAA 063 THE AMERICAN INDIAN WARS 1860–90
0850452597 MAA 067 THE INDIAN MUTINY
0850452759 MAA 072 NORTH-WEST FRONTIER 1837–1947
0850453070 MAA 092 INDIAN INFANTRY REGIMENTS 1860–1914
0850453356 MAA 095 THE BOXER REBELLION
1855328380 MAA 107 BRITISH INFANTRY EQUIPMENTS (1)
184176471X MAA 138 BRITISH CAVALRY EQUIPMENTS 1800–1941
                    (REVISED ED)
0850456088 MAA 163 THE AMERICAN PLAINS INDIANS
0850456096 MAA 168 US CAVALRY ON THE PLAINS 1850–90
0850456843 MAA 173 THE ALAMO AND THE WAR OF TEXAN
                    INDEPENDENCE 1835–36
0850457386 MAA 186 THE APACHES
0850457939 MAA 193 THE BRITISH ARMY ON CAMPAIGN (1) 1816–53
0850458277 MAA 196 THE BRITISH ARMY ON CAMPAIGN (2) 1854–56
0850458498 MAA 201 THE BRITISH ARMY ON CAMPAIGN (4)
                    1882–1902
085045901X MAA 212 QUEEN VICTORIA'S ENEMIES (1) SOUTH AFRICA
0850459370 MAA 215 QUEEN VICTORIA'S ENEMIES (2)
                    NORTH AFRICA
0850459435 MAA 219 QUEEN VICTORIA'S ENEMIES (3) INDIA
0850451973 MAA 226 THE AMERICAN WAR 1812–14
1855321033 MAA 230 THE US ARMY 1890–1920
1855321211 MAA 233 FRENCH ARMY 1870–71 FRANCO-PRUSSIAN
                    WAR (1) IMPERIAL TROOPS
1855321351 MAA 237 FRENCH ARMY 1870–71 FRANCO-PRUSSIAN
                    WAR (2) REPUBLICAN TROOPS
185532430X MAA 272 THE MEXICAN ADVENTURE 1861–67
185532346X MAA 275 THE TAIPING REBELLION 1851–66
1855323710 MAA 277 THE RUSSO-TURKISH WAR 1877
1855323893 MAA 281 US DRAGOONS 1833–55
1855325667 MAA 288 AMERICAN INDIANS OF THE SOUTHEAST
1855326000 MAA 294 BRITISH FORCES IN THE WEST INDIES
                    1793–1815
1855326205 MAA 299 AUSTRIAN AUXILIARY TROOPS 1792–1816
1855326124 MAA 301 THE BOER WARS (1) 1836–96
1855326132 MAA 303 THE BOER WARS (2) 1898–1902
1855328011 MAA 323 THE AUSTRIAN ARMY 1836–66 (1) INFANTRY
1855327627 MAA 324 THE NORTH-EAST FRONTIER 1837–1901
1855328003 MAA 329 THE AUSTRIAN ARMY 1836–66 (2) CAVALRY
185532878X MAA 344 TRIBES OF THE SIOUX NATION
184176051X MAA 345 UNITED STATES ARMY 1812–15

To order any of these titles, or for more information on Osprey Publishing, contact:

Osprey Direct (UK)   *Tel:* +44 (0)1933 443863   *Fax:* +44 (0)1933 443849   *E-mail:* info@ospreydirect.co.uk
Osprey Direct (USA) c/o MBI Publishing   *Toll-free:* 1 800 826 6600   *Phone:* 1 715 294 3345
Fax: 1 715 294 4448   *E-mail:* info@ospreydirectusa.com
www.ospreypublishing.com

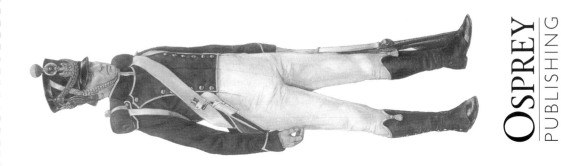

FIND OUT MORE ABOUT OSPREY

❏ Please send me the latest listing of Osprey's publications

❏ I would like to subscribe to Osprey's e-mail newsletter

Title / rank

Name

Address

City / county

Postcode / zip   state / country

e-mail

I am interested in:

❏ Ancient world
❏ Medieval world
❏ 16th century
❏ 17th century
❏ 18th century
❏ Napoleonic
❏ 19th century

❏ American Civil War
❏ World War 1
❏ World War 2
❏ Modern warfare
❏ Military aviation
❏ Naval warfare

Please send to:

USA & Canada:
Osprey Direct USA, c/o MBI Publishing, P.O. Box 1, 729 Prospect Avenue, Osceola, WI 54020

UK, Europe and rest of world:
Osprey Direct UK, P.O. Box 140, Wellingborough, Northants, NN8 2FA, United Kingdom

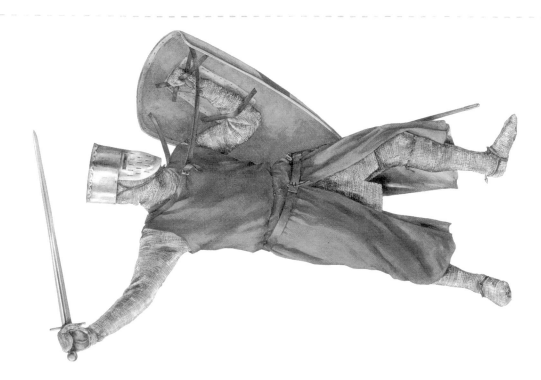

OSPREY
PUBLISHING

www.ospreypublishing.com

call our telephone hotline
for a free information pack

USA & Canada: 1-800-826-6600
UK, Europe and rest of world call:
+44 (0) 1933 443 863

Young Guardsman
Figure taken from *Warrior 22:
Imperial Guardsman 1799–1815*
Published by Osprey
Illustrated by Christa Hook

POSTCARD

Knight, c.1190
Figure taken from *Warrior 1: Norman Knight 950 – 1204AD*
Published by Osprey
Illustrated by Christa Hook

www.ospreypublishing.com